BOOKS BY

JOHN SWARTZWELDER

THE TIME MACHINE DID IT (2004)

DOUBLE WONDERFUL (2005)

HOW I CONQUERED YOUR PLANET (2006)

THE EXPLODING DETECTIVE (2007)

DEAD MEN SCARE ME STUPID (2008)

EARTH VS. EVERYBODY (2009)

THE EXPLODING DETECTIVE

JOHN SWARTZWELDER

Kennydale Books
Chatsworth, California

Copyright © 2007
by John Swartzwelder

Published by:
Kennydale Books
P.O. Box 3925
Chatsworth, California 91313-3925

All Rights Reserved. No part of this book may be reproduced or transmitted in any form or by any means, electronic or mechanical, including photocopying, recording or by any information storage and retrieval system, without written permission from the author, except for the inclusion of brief quotations in a review.

First Printing February, 2007
Second Printing December, 2009

ISBN 13 (paperback edition) 978-0-9755799-6-1
ISBN 13 (hardback edition) 978-0-9755799-7-8
ISBN 10 (paperback edition) 0-9755799-6-7
ISBN 10 (hardback edition) 0-9755799-7-5

Library of Congress Control Number: 2007900417

This book is a work of fiction. Names, characters, places and incidents either are the product of the author's imagination or are used fictitiously, and any resemblance to actual persons, living or dead, events, or locales is entirely coincidental.

Printed in the United States of America

CHAPTER ONE

I suppose the first thing I should do is apologize for the billions of dead. And that I do. Humbly. And sincerely. When a man has done something wrong, I feel, it's that man's duty to own up to it. And I do. I'd apologize more fully, but I'm falling off a cliff right now.

They say a human body can't fall at more than 120 miles per hour, but that's because they've never met me. Of course, I had a jet pack on my back. And rockets.

This was my first test run with some new equipment I'd just bought, and so far it wasn't working out as well as the advertisements had promised. Instead of streaking through the sky like a bolt of lightning, I was whistling down the side of a cliff like a sack of cement.

The ground was coming up at me pretty fast, but I consoled myself with the knowledge that the ground was more afraid of me than I was of it. I read that in an article somewhere. But I was still worried. There were boulders down there too. And boulders aren't afraid of anything. (Same article.) The good news was that this all might be just a dream. The bad news was that of course it wasn't.

It pays to stay calm in these kinds of situations. Ask any test pilot. You're supposed to just relax, take it easy, calmly access your situation, then come up with the right answer. Right now. Really fast. It's that easy. I calmly ran down a mental checklist of all the things I needed to do in the next eight seconds. The first thing on the list was to try to cut down my speed somehow, because my nose was starting to burn like a blow torch as I approached Mach 1. I figured the quickest way to slow down would be to take off my jet pack and throw it away. So I started undoing the straps.

I managed to get the first strap loose—and I know what you're thinking: he's half way there—but the loose strap caused the jet pack to slide over to one side and begin propelling me in a different direction, away from the ground, which I was just about to hit, and towards a riverbank full of alligators and African natives with spears. The fact that the spears were made of rubber, and the alligators were members of the Screen Actors Guild and were at that moment arguing with the director over the sound an alligator makes, didn't make them any less frightening. Avoiding the alligators now moved to the top of my list of things to do.

The jet pack had slid down to the small of my back by now and there was no way I could reach back there and switch off the engine. I tried anyway, twisting myself around just enough to destabilize the whole machine. I spun around in a circle, then shot straight up into the sky. Then I roared back down at the alligators again, causing several of them to faint, and one of them to walk off the picture.

For the next twenty minutes my flight path gyrated wildly, from the ground to the clouds then back towards the ground again. One minute I would be banging on the passenger window of an airliner motioning for some old lady to let me in, the next I would be half flying, half running, over the rapids of the Central City River, dragging fishing poles and determined fishermen behind me. I guess I must have been quite a sight. Everywhere I flew I kept hearing: "Now I've seen everything!" and then a gunshot.

Finally I managed to reach the throttle control on the jet pack and shut the engine down. I was only a few feet off the ground at this point, so I dug my heels into the dirt to try to slow myself down, somehow managing to dislodge a huge rock, which began rolling after me.

I started to run, with the rock right behind me and gaining fast. At the last moment, I managed to avoid it by diving into a pit. A pit full of rocks! I screamed and screamed and screamed.

While all this was going on, an unusual crime was taking place in Central City's industrial district.

Strange looking people with blank expressions on their faces were breaking into warehouses and chemical plants, ignoring the money and other valuables they found and, instead, hauling out dyes, pigments, polyvinylchloride, Styrofoam, chemical abrasives, and corrugated cardboard. They didn't seem to mind that a large crowd of people had gathered to watch them, or that half the Central City police force was shooting at them. They just kept stealing.

The policemen's bullets didn't seem to have any effect on the robbers at all. They just bounced off them. A few onlookers borrowed the policemen's guns to take a crack at it themselves, but they couldn't do any better. There seemed to be no stopping these strange thieves.

Occasionally they would stop on their own accord, adopt a listening attitude, then change direction and begin loading other items onto their trucks. The police stood by picking their noses helplessly, while the crowd pressed closer, picking their noses with interest.

Just when the strange criminals were loading up the last of the trucks, I crashed into the middle of the street from twenty thousand feet. I had finished my disastrous test flight and was on my disastrous way home. The startled criminals scattered, leaving their booty behind, and the police took off after them, baying like bloodhounds.

I was pretty badly smashed up, and my clothes were covered with all kinds of debris from my flight: bits of broken tree branches, fishing poles, "No Trespassing" signs, a couple of monkeys from the zoo, and some library books. I looked like an old dumpster someone had set on fire.

The crowd's resentment of my intrusion changed quickly to interest when they realized how horrific my crash was, and how badly I was hurt. I wasn't as interesting as the crime they had been witnessing, but I was something. Everyone crowded around. Some even resumed picking their noses.

"Don't move him," cautioned one member of the crowd.

"I thought you were supposed to move them," said another.

"Well, don't move him too far, that's my point."

When I had regained consciousness, and they had finally stopped moving me—I was 150 yards away by then—they asked who I was and what my dramatic entrance was all about. That was my cue. I started fishing charred business cards out of my smoldering pockets and handing them around.

The cards proclaimed that I was "THE FLYING DETECTIVE." They were actually just my regular cards that say "DETECTIVE." I had written "THE FLYING" in with a pencil. No point in throwing away all those old cards I had.

I was starting to interest the crowd very much. Not only was I severely hurt, and might die, but I appeared to be some kind of super hero. There had never been any super heroes in our town before. They didn't know why. There just hadn't. They plied me with questions. What powers did I have? Super heroes, as they understood it, had special powers. What did I have going for me?

I informed them that I was not a super hero.

But I was the next best thing. I was a licensed private detective—with a difference. The difference being that I was jet-propelled. That meant I could solve their cases for them at supersonic speed, so there would be less waiting. And at a bargain price, so they'd have some money left.

"Aren't you that Frank Burly who works over on Third Avenue?" someone asked me. "That guy nobody likes?"

"Well, yes and no," I told him. I was Frank Burly, of course, but I was under the impression that a lot of people liked me. That I was quite popular. So the answer had to be "yes and no" there.

The crowd was beginning to lose interest in me now. They had thought I might be some kind of superhuman being. Apparently I wasn't. I was just an ordinary human, the same as you and me. They had seen people like you and me before. Lots of times. A few people started to drift away and look for a different crowd to be in, one that had found something more interesting.

One guy was still a little interested in me. He examined my card again, then raised his hand. "I don't like my neighbor. Can you get rid of him for me?"

A guy on the other side of the crowd looked at him in horror. "Hey, I'm your neighbor."

The first guy glanced at his neighbor, then looked back at me. "I was thinking maybe you could vaporize him with your eyeballs or something."

"Say, look, Fred…" began the neighbor.

I told the man that The Flying Detective would be glad to look into his problem for him, though his vaporizing idea was out. I had no super powers. I thought I had just made that clear. But something could probably be done. Just call the number on the card and we could set up an appointment.

Then I prepared to make my dramatic exit, blasting off into the unknown, from whence I came. Unfortunately, I couldn't get my jet pack going. One of the crash landings I had made on the way to this crash landing must have dinged up something important. I kicked it, to see if that would do anything. It did. It started a fuel leak in the engine and a small fire on one of my legs. I kicked it again. More leaks. More leg fires.

I got out my tool kit and started fiddling with the engine. Some of the more handy guys in the crowd tried to give me pointers, but I told them to just let me do it. I can do it. Just melt back into the crowd and leave this to me.

After a half hour had gone by with no more talking, just hammering, cursing, and wrenching, the crowd began to disperse. An hour later so did I. I never could get the damn thing going, so I had to walk home. It wasn't a very good advertisement for how fast I was.

CHAPTER TWO

Everyone without talent has to have a gimmick. It had taken me a long time to learn that. I had spent my entire career watching detectives around me becoming rich and famous and internationally respected, while I had trouble making my rent each month. And all because the other detectives had talent and I had none. It didn't seem fair to me.

Maybe, I thought, this was something the government should fix, the way they fix everything else. I sent a letter to them suggesting this, and they said they'd get right on it. And while they were working on it, they suggested, I could pass the time by voting for them. But the months went by and the problem wasn't fixed. Then, not long before the epic first flight you have just read about, I stumbled on the answer to my problem. I found the perfect gimmick. A gimmick that would propel me to the top of my profession at 800 miles per hour. A jet pack.

I found it in the back of a copy of 2nd Rate Detective Stories magazine, which I was reading in the hopes of picking up some 2nd rate professional tips. It was an old Himmelbitter ("Heaven Biter") Mark 2 that had been built during the fading moments of World War II—built with a very specific purpose in mind.

In early 1945, the advertisement breathlessly revealed, the Nazis were starting to have premonitions of their own deaths as the Allied army got closer, so they began making preparations to go to Heaven and take it over. They planned to take out St. Peter with long range atomic cannons, blast open The Pearly Gates with gelignite, then swarm through the clouds with jet packs, running down the angels and forcing them to work for their new German-speaking "Creators." The ad didn't say whether their plan worked out or not, but I'm guessing it didn't. My prayers aren't answered very often, but when they are it isn't in German.

The Heaven Biter that was for sale had been completely rebuilt, the ad said, and was guaranteed to "Fly Faster Than The Angels," a claim which took on an ominous tone when you knew the whole story. Still, you like to have guarantees for things like this.

When the jet pack arrived I was amazed at how heavy it was for how small it was. They really knew how to build 'em in those days. Or maybe they didn't. Maybe that's why it was heavier. Maybe if they'd known how to build it, it wouldn't have been so heavy.

For additional thrust during takeoff, I added a couple of small rockets I found in a women's fashion magazine. That was bad ad placement, it seemed to me. Still, they got their sale. So I guess they knew what they were doing. I guess that's why they're in the advertising business and I'm not.

My first test of the jet pack didn't work out very well, as you have just read, so I decided to do a little practicing before I launched myself into the public eye again. The public expects professionals to know how to use their equipment. You don't expect dentists, for example, to be torn to shreds by their own drills or smothered by their own smocks, or baseball players to get caught in their own mitts. You expect them to know how to use their equipment properly. Same thing with flying detectives and their equipment.

I went out to a vacant lot near my office and set up a plywood criminal to apprehend, then fired up my jet pack and started the countdown on my rockets. I understand why I blew up. I had a hundred gallons of jet fuel on my back. But why did the plywood criminal explode? And where did the vacant lot go?

They say any crash you can walk away from is a good crash, though I've never heard anyone involved in the crash say that. It's just the people across the street who say stuff like that. I'm not even sure why we're listening to them. They can't even see very well from over there. Anyway, I'm glad to say I walked away from that one.

"Is there a fireman in the house?" I asked passersby. "Anyone know how to put me out?"

A couple of young men walking by thought

they knew what to do in a situation like this. They confidently set to work putting out the fire.

It took them awhile to extinguish all the flames, because they had to make sure none of the sparks in my crotch flared up again. They must have stamped on that fire for twenty minutes. But they finally got it out to their satisfaction. As they were leaving, I remembered the two men. They were a couple of bullies from my high school who never had liked me. It was nice to see they didn't hold any grudges.

I made some adjustments to my equipment when I got home from the hospital. The instructions were in German, so I could only guess at what they said. In fact, I'm only guessing they were in German. Then I took another practice run.

After I was released from the Emergency Burn Unit, and the doctors said I could go home if I didn't move around too much or overly excite myself, I decided I was ready.

I began making daily patrols over the city— partly to look for crimes that needed solving and potential clients who might need my help, but mostly to advertise my business. I figured once people saw me up there soaring through the clouds, they wouldn't be satisfied with ordinary detectives anymore. They would want one that could fly.

Unfortunately, my daily patrols weren't so much patrols as they were a series of spectacular air tragedies, reminding some old timers of the Hindenburg, others of the Akron. I don't think I've slid down the sides of so many buildings in my life. Or skidded along so many sidewalks on my belly. But with each flight I got a little better at adjusting my altitude, speed, and general direction. All of these factors are important when you are jet-propelled and covered in rockets.

I was glad I had added the rockets. The rocket assisted takeoffs not only increased my speed, they made the whole thing more exciting. There was an explosion when I took off and another one when I arrived, so it was like I was a magician or something. It was such a dazzling effect people seldom noticed the blood running down my face.

These initial flights didn't get me any business, but they did attract attention. A local supermarket tabloid newspaper was the first to do a feature story about me. "He Flies!!!!" screamed their banner headline. The next day a slightly smaller headline said: "He Still Flies." And a week later a story on page three was headlined: "Still flying. Day 6." A couple of days later the story was back on the front page: "Another Flying Man!" showing that same picture of me. Finally they contacted me and asked if I could do anything else besides fly. Something new. Their readers already knew about my flying. They wanted something fresh from me. Swimming, maybe. I told them my job was battling the dark forces, not helping them fill up their newspaper. They said they didn't get it.

After that, I didn't get any publicity at all, except when something went wrong with one of my flights. "Flying Detective In Flagpole Drama," "Flying Detective Fouls City's Windshields," and "Flying Detective Clinging To Life—Again," are a few headlines that I remember. Oh well, as long as they spell your name right, as Hitler said.

Despite all my promotional flights, I wasn't getting any business. Nobody seemed to need or want a jet-propelled detective. I was starting to think that maybe I should have checked out the market for such a concept before I started investing my time and money so heavily in it. I was starting to think I might have picked the wrong gimmick. Maybe I should have gone with that other idea I had—those stilts. But it turns out I needn't have worried. My gimmick was about to pay off big-time, in a way I hadn't expected.

Those strange criminals, whose robbery I had accidentally broken up on my first test flight, had returned for another try. But this time they weren't unsupervised as they had been before. They had a leader now. He was a dead ringer for Napoleon Bonaparte. And he ran the operation like a pro. No wasted motions. No diversions. And, above all, no panicking when something unexpected, like me, happened.

The police arrived on the scene quickly, but couldn't do anything to stop the robbery. Under "Napoleon's" direction, some of the robbers advanced to attack the police in the center, then wheeled and took out first one flank, then the other.

"The Battle of Austerlitz, begorra!" said one historical minded cop, as he was being outflanked.

With the police forces badly scattered, and now arguing among themselves over whether it was

The Battle of Austerlitz or The Battle of the Three Emperors, the robbers quickly finished loading up their trucks and drove away. Total elapsed time for the whole operation—less than thirty minutes. And not one of the raiders had been killed or captured.

The police were stunned. They knew they weren't geniuses—geniuses didn't apply for jobs at the police station, they walked right past it—but they weren't used to being so easily outmaneuvered. Police psychiatrists had to work overtime for days straightening the policemen out.

The public was fascinated by this raid. For one thing, only chemicals were stolen, when the company payroll was there for the taking. And the robbers themselves were even more intriguing: with their expressionless faces, the mechanical way they went about their business, the RC antennas and smoke stacks some of them had, and the way they would occasionally stop to change each others' batteries, or take their heads off and use them to bang open a crate. These weren't the kinds of robbers Central City usually got. These robbers were something new.

But the thing that fascinated, and vaguely worried, the public most, was the presence of Napoleon Bonaparte at the head of this criminal gang. It had been their impression that Napoleon was dead, and had been dead since 1821. With everything else they had to worry about in their daily lives, they didn't expect to have to worry about dead guys too.

The tabloids had a field day, of course. "Dead

Midget Menaces Central City!" "Frenchmen Won't Stay Dead!" and "Everybody From 1821 Returning From Grave!" were some of the milder headlines.

Apparently emboldened by his success, "Napoleon" began raiding Central City's industrial district on an almost daily basis. Soon, businesses in the area stopped bothering to unload their shipments. They just left them on their pallets outside for the raiders to pick up. It saved time. They could go out of business faster that way.

The police did their best, but there was nothing they could do to stop the raids. Napoleon not only outmanned and outgunned them, he outmaneuvered them every time. He made monkeys out of them. And nobody likes paying big tax dollars to be protected by monkeys. Nobody does. Complaints about the lack of adequate protection began flooding into City Hall.

Mayor Happy Safeton (born Pernell Slyme), who had just been elected on his promise to "Keep Our Town Safe And Happy With Happy Safeton" (a slogan that had fascinated voters because of its cleverness and double—some said triple— meaning), was very unhappy. A crime wave like this made his administration look bad. It made a mockery of his slogan. He wasn't going to get re-elected if this kept up. And it wasn't even his fault. It was the Police Commissioner's fault.

He stormed into Police Commissioner Brenner's office, waving a fistful of citizen's complaints and demanded the Commissioner do something about the whole mess. The Commissioner said he would, and promptly stormed into the Police Chief's office and yelled at him. And so on. Eventually somebody stormed into my office, and I went and yelled at the old guy who ran the elevator. I don't know who he yelled at, but I do know that eventually the buck ended up being passed back to the Mayor, which didn't make him happy at all.

Everybody in town was demanding action, but nobody knew what to do. Then one day they got an idea. The idea they got was me.

It happened during one of Napoleon's daily raids. Just as the last getaway truck was pulling away, loaded with propylene oxide, red dye #6 and lithium batteries, I suddenly fell out of the sky from 4000 feet and exploded in front of the truck, tipping it over. The creatures inside the truck got away, but the cargo was saved.

A crowd quickly gathered around my smoking remains.

"Hey! It's the Exploding Detective!" said one wag.

"Flying Detective," I corrected him, slowly and painfully rising to my feet—though I had to admit his description of what I did was better than mine.

Everybody was surprised to see that I had survived the fall, and the explosion, and the truck rolling over onto me, and all the people in the crowd stepping on me so they could see better, but I'd been hurt a lot worse than that before. I guess they thought they were dealing with an amateur.

I groggily looked around for the letters I had been taking to the post office, but most of them had been incinerated in the blast. Grumbling, I walked over and laid down on a gurney and waited for my life to be saved.

My spectacular foiling of the big robbery caused much excited comment and speculation around town over the next few days. Who was this Flying Detective anyway, they wondered. What was his story?

Everybody had seen me around, of course. I was nothing new. In fact, nearly a tenth of the population had stamped me out at one time or another. But a growing number of people were beginning to think that I might be something more than I appeared to be. The way they had it figured out, any normal man who flew like I did would have been dead long ago. And yet I still lived. Maybe I wasn't just some old idiot in a jet pack. Maybe I was secretly a genuine super hero, with super powers that would make your eyes pop out. After all, didn't Clark Kent and Bruce Wayne seem like blundering fools? And didn't they always deny being super heroes? And yet they were the greatest of them all. That might be what was happening here, too. It was the only thing that made sense, when you thought about it in a certain way, and overlooked a few things.

The newspapers picked up on this idea and expanded on it, not only speculating about my super powers, but actually confirming them, and listing them. The Tribune said I could run faster and jump higher than lightning, and crush a piece of coal into whatever you want. The Chronicle said I could out-smart a battleship. The Post said I was half man, half rattlesnake, and half nuclear bomb, explaining that I was the happy result of a man and a snake screwing a box of dynamite. These sensational new revelations about me greatly excited the public.

You're probably wondering what I thought of all this super hero stuff. Actually, I hadn't heard anything about it. I had been in the observation ward at the hospital since my most recent crash and had just gotten out. I noticed people were looking at me strangely all the way home on the bus, but I assumed it was because of the bones that were sticking out of my cheek.

When I got to my office I decided to sit down and take stock of my situation. It was time for me to figure out, in actual dollars and cents, exactly how this Flying Detective gimmick of mine was working out so far. When I totaled everything up, I was staggered. The numbers were staggering. I was losing a staggering amount of money. I was doing even worse as The Flying Detective than I was as Frank Burly.

I ran the numbers again, and now I was doing even worse! I decided that that was it. I wasn't going to run those numbers ever again. And I was going to send the jet pack back to Nazi Germany tomorrow. No more gimmicks for me. I was through being The Flying Detective.

As I made this decision and was starting to erase "Flying" from my business cards, letterheads, and complimentary calendars, my door opened and two men walked in. It was the Mayor of Central City and the Police

Commissioner. I wondered what I'd done now, and if I should make a run for it.

"How do you do, Mr. Burly," said the Mayor. "I'm Happy Safeton. Perhaps you've voted for me."

"Nah."

His smile tailed off a little, then rallied back. "I understand you're a super hero, with powers and abilities beyond my understanding."

"Who told you that?"

"Everyone told me. We all know about it. It's true, isn't it? You can tell me. I'm the Mayor."

Before I could think of a nice way to tell a Mayor that he's stupid—while I was still trying to remember what Emily Post had said about that—Commissioner Brenner broke into the conversation: "There's a job in it for you if you are a super hero."

"Huh?"

"Yes," said the Mayor, "We're looking for someone to save Central City."

"From what?"

"From the gang that's been terrorizing the industrial district. And from this nut case who's been leading the raids who thinks he's Napoleon."

"At what rate of payment?"

"What?"

"How much does this job you're talking about pay?"

The two men were taken aback by this question.

"We naturally assumed," said the Mayor, "that a genuine super hero would do this for the honor of the thing. For the Truth and the Justice involved."

"That isn't my business model," I replied. "I want Truth, Justice, and $1,500 a week."

The Mayor and Commissioner Brenner exchanged glances, then excused themselves and moved off a ways to discuss the matter in private. I ambled over in their direction, pretending I was straightening a plant, so I could listen in.

"$1,500!" said the Mayor. "That's more than I pay my nephew!"

"You don't have a nephew," said Brenner.

"What's that got to do with anything?"

"And this guy isn't a super hero."

"What do you mean?"

"Well, look at him. He's fat and stupid, and he's not even that strong. When we shook hands, I should have been the one that yelped in pain, not him. He's just some clown with a jet pack."

"The papers say he's a super hero."

"The papers say we're honest."

The Mayor's excited smile faded a little. "Hey, yeah, that's right." He thought for a moment. "Well it doesn't matter anyway. Maybe he's a super hero, maybe he's not. But either way, the public wants him. If we get him on our team and he succeeds, we can take a lot of the credit. If he fails, he can take the heat alone."

The Commissioner looked at him with respect. Happy Safeton (Pernell Slyme) hadn't made it all the way to the Mayor's Office on his good looks and charm.

"That makes sense," he admitted.

The Mayor noticed I was very close to them now, pretending to wash the windows. "Should we be talking in front of him?"

Brenner considered me for a moment, then nodded. "Sure. He probably doesn't understand most of what we're saying anyway."

He was wrong about that. I didn't understand all of the multi-syllable words, of course. But I got the gist of what they were saying. They were saying something about me. Finally they finished their discussion and turned back to me.

"All right," said the Mayor. "$1,500 a week, minus the usual 10% agent's commission for Commissioner Brenner and myself, of course."

This confused me. "Are you guys agents too?"

"We're everything that gets paid," said Brenner.

"Oh, I see."

The Mayor looked around my office. "Where's your super hero costume? You don't fly around in a suit and tie, do you?"

"It's at the cleaners."

"Oh, I see. Well then, I'll hold off the press conference about you until next week. Will your costume be back by then?"

"Sure."

"Excellent! Welcome aboard, Mr. Burly. Or should I say Mr. The Flying Detective! From now on, Central City is entirely in your capable hands."

I shook their hands. "When do I get a check?"

"When you've done some work," said Brenner.

"Fine."

CHAPTER THREE

When people start calling you a super hero, you don't look at yourself in the mirror the same way anymore. Now you look at yourself in the mirror and say: "Are super heroes supposed to look like that?" And you're not sure. But you don't think so.

I got a pile of old comic books and started making notes about what super heroes were supposed to look like—their costumes, hairstyles, any special crime-fighting gadgets they might carry around with them, and so on.

Their costumes, I found, were pretty varied. Some super heroes wore red, some blue. Some had capes, others cowls. They all had one thing in common, however. All of their costumes looked like long underwear. I didn't like this. I didn't particularly want to parade around the streets in my union suit, with kids and old women giving me the horselaugh. But, in any kind of business, you've got to give the public what it wants. And in the super hero business, the public wants underpants.

Borrowing design elements from all of the super heroes, and adding a few personal touches of my own, I designed a costume that, in my opinion, was as good as any of them. It was bright orange, like an explosion, with a blue shield. In the center of the shield were the initials "TFD" (The Flying Detective), along with the smaller initials "TM" (trademark). I decided on a cape, like Superman's, because it drew attention away from the fact that I was practically naked. The whole thing looked pretty damned impressive to me when I finished the design. A local costume shop said they could have it made up for me in a couple of days, if I was sure I really wanted it. So that was taken care of.

As for the crime-fighting gadgets I might need, once again the comic books were indispensable. I sent away for a set of Junior Grappling Hooks, an Instant Disguise Kit ("Just put face in box"), Disappearing Handcuffs, and X-Ray Glasses, so I could see through criminal women's clothes. I also sent away for a 24 week course that would, once I had mastered the special techniques involved, allow me to throw my voice through a steel door. Total cost for the whole getup? Maybe ninety bucks. I could afford that now, easy.

Unfortunately, when the gadgets arrived they didn't work as well as the comic books and I had hoped. The X-ray glasses didn't work at all at first because I had them on backwards. I couldn't see anything and everybody could see into my head. I took them off and stuck them in my back pocket. Now they could all see up my ass. I threw them away. The Instant Disguise Kit just tore my face up something awful. And I lost the disappearing handcuffs the first day. I decided that maybe I'd better be one of those super heroes who doesn't have any gadgets.

I went down to City Hall to show the Mayor and the Police Commissioner my costume and let them know that I was ready to go, and was officially on the clock.

"Wonderful!" enthused the Mayor, as he looked over my costume. "You look like Superman, or Batman, or... god dammit, you look like everybody!"

"There's a price tag on your cape," said the Commissioner.

I took it off.

"Now, is there anything you need?" asked the Mayor. "Or are you ready to start saving us right now?"

I said I was all set, but suggested the Police Commissioner might want to install a "Flying Detective Signal" in his office. That way, he could shine a smiling outline of me in the sky that could be seen all over the city when he needed my services—when he couldn't handle his job himself. The Commissioner was dubious. Those 16,000 watt signals, he told me, cost money. Plus, he didn't particularly want to advertise his incompetence all over the city. Enough people knew about that already without putting it up in lights. But the Mayor thought it was a crackerjack idea. The signal would be installed at once.

"Do you have a catchphrase?" asked the

Mayor. "Like 'Up, Up, And Away!' or something like that? We'll need it for our press releases about you."

"'Up, Up, And Away' sounds good," I said.

"No, you can't use that. It's taken."

"How about 'Up, Down, And Away'? Anybody got that?"

The Mayor and the Commissioner exchanged glances.

"I don't think you need a catchphrase," said Brenner.

"Fine."

"Gilding the lily," agreed the Mayor.

"Gotcha."

The next day was the day of the big press conference. The Mayor introduced me to the roomful of reporters, with a cleverly worded disclaimer that seemed to say that I was his personal discovery and best friend if all this worked out well, but that if it didn't, he had never heard of me, and could prove it. Then he nudged me up to the microphones.

There was tremendous applause. The media was plainly all fired up. They had heard a lot about me, from themselves. I was barraged with questions.

"What super powers will you be using to protect our city?"

"Uh... all of them."

"What is your costume made out of? Why does it look so new?"

"Wool."

"Do you need a sidekick? I could be Newspaper Boy."

"Next question."

"What is your favorite crime?"

"Murder, I guess."

I answered all of their questions as well as I could, but I'm not much of a public speaker, and I don't know the answers to too many questions, so pretty soon the press conference started to drag a little. At the one hour mark, a couple of reporters in the back started to go to sleep. Awhile later, so did I.

The Mayor heard the snores and decided it was time to wind up the press conference. He began handing out slick press information packets about me. Each packet contained my bio, pictures of my father (a rattlesnake) and my mother (a box of dynamite), a list of the worlds I had already saved, (I never even heard of some of them. Where's "Benny"?), and publicity photos of me posing before an American flag, taking the Central City Oath, and a gag photo that made it look like the Mayor and I were friends.

The reporters snapped up the packets eagerly. Some even had me autograph them, saying it wasn't for them, it was for some smaller reporter. I graciously complied with all these requests, adding "Up, Down, And Away!" to some of the signatures. So, all in all, my first press conference ended up being a rousing success.

Then the Mayor hustled me over to a TV studio so that everyone in Central City could see me. I'm told that my TV interview was almost as boring as my press conference. Something about charisma. Too much charisma, I think they said.

"Our viewers want to know," the interviewer began, "the source of your great powers. Are you from a different planet?"

"Yes, I am from a different planet, Lyle."

"Were you ever bitten by a radioactive insect?"

"Yes, Lyle, I was."

"Did ancient Gods give you your powers?"

"Uh huh."

"Do you come from a race of super heroes?"

"Yeah."

"So... you got your super powers from just about everyplace then."

"Pretty much. Are these fruits on the table here decorative? Or can I eat these?"

"Decorative."

"Fine."

"Now, our stagehands have set up some things here in the studio to allow you to demonstrate your super powers for our audience: a lump of coal you can squeeze into a diamond, a steel girder you can melt with the heat from your eyeballs, and a convicted felon for you to disintegrate. Are you ready, Mr. Flying Detective?"

"Uh... actually, Lyle, I feel I should save my super strength for my fight against evil."

"Oh. I see. Well then... I told you you couldn't eat those."

"Oh, okay."

"They're wax."

"Fine."

When the interview was over, the Mayor said

he thought that was enough public appearances for me for one day. I was glad. I wasn't looking forward to that three hour concert at the stadium anyway. As we were leaving, he said the next time I was asked how I got my super powers, I should just say I got them by voting for him. I said I would.

Now, you would think, wouldn't you, that a super hero could sleep in as long as he wanted in the morning. A guy like that should be able to make his own hours, I would have thought. I was informed that this was not so late the next morning. I was awakened by a loud banging on my door at around eleven o'clock.

When I opened the door I found the Police Commissioner and Mayor Safeton standing on my doorstep, pointing at their watches.

A half hour later I was in costume, standing on a street corner, yawning, and keeping a bleary eye out for crime.

I quickly attracted a lot of attention. Everyone stopped to gawk at my costume and check out my superness for themselves. They felt my muscles, punched me experimentally in the stomach, jabbed me in the side with pen knives, and so on. I had anticipated this, so I was wearing a great many extra pairs of underwear under my costume. This not only cut down on the pain, it also made me look stronger than I really am.

Some of the people in the crowd wanted to see me demonstrate my super human strength for them by wrecking something. Fortunately, wrecking stuff doesn't require super powers. Not if you're clumsy enough. I could wreck things

Superman would have had trouble with. It's genetic, I guess. My grandfather wrecked North Dakota without doing anything. Honestly. He was just standing there.

So I ripped mirrors off of parked cars, knocked over stop signs just by leaning on them, derailed a trolley, even broke a guy's leg. The crowd was amazed. I was kind of amazed too. I'm always amazed when I destroy something without any effort. It just shows what you can do if you're not balanced properly.

Little kids were fascinated by me. They were always coming up to me wanting me to crush things for them—their homework or their little sister—or to sign autographs for them. I did whatever crushing they wanted done, but I told them the autographs would cost them $150 each. I was a big-shot now, I informed them. The value of my signature had gone up. And the expense would have to be passed onto them, the nation's kids. Otherwise the economy wouldn't work. The ones who already had my autograph were pleased about this. The value of their collections had just gone through the roof. The rest of them thought it was bullshit, though they couldn't say so until they were older.

But I didn't get to stand around looking pretty all day. There was work to be done, the Mayor informed me. He said I wasn't just there to protect the city from super villains. $1,500 bought more than that, even these days. I was there to protect the city period. He said I should re-read my contract if there was any confusion about this. I was getting kind of bored just standing around anyway, so I started patrolling the city—crashing into small time crooks, sliding sideways through gambling dens and auction houses, getting dead cats down from trees, changing street lights that had burned out, and so on.

The police liked this new arrangement since it gave them more time to relax. Pretty soon the only place you could find a policeman was on the lawn chairs set up outside of the police station. All the actual crime busting was left up to me.

Since I had so much to do, the Mayor decided I should have a sidekick, so he assigned one of his younger staff members, a wise-cracking go-getter named Smitty to me. But I had to spend too much time saying: "Quiet, Smitty." So I finally fired him.

I wasn't very good at being a super hero at first. I know it sounds easy, and the comic books make it look easy, but it's not. I didn't know how to do a lot of the things super heroes are supposed to know how to do.

You're expected to stand there and let bullets bounce off your chest, for example. This is hard to do. All my extra pairs of underwear I was wearing helped, and some of the bullets did, in fact, bounce off. But most of them didn't. I was usually up half the night picking bullet-heads out of my chest with tweezers. I was also expected to dodge the empty guns that were thrown at my head after all the bullets had been fired. That wasn't easy either. Some of those criminals have good arms.

The Mayor liked seeing the bullets bounce off me. That proved that I was for real. He even took a few shots at me himself to show how I worked to some of his buddies from City Hall. Once again, the empty gun nearly took my head off. But I didn't mind. You've got to keep the boss happy, if you want to keep those big paychecks coming in.

Another thing I was expected to be able to do was to crash through walls and bang people's heads together. I couldn't even get all the way through most of those walls. Usually a fire-truck would have to come and get me out. And almost every time I banged two heads together, one of them turned out to be mine, and the other turned out to be the Mayor's. I've got to work on that. There must be some trick to it.

Still, I managed to do a fairly decent job as Central City's resident super hero, mostly due to the fearsome reputation the newspapers had given me. I'd streak out of the sky or skid along the sidewalk on my belly towards the scene of a crime and more often than not the criminals would take off before I'd even arrived. So I managed to keep the peace without doing too much actual fighting.

As the days passed, I became a familiar sight on the streets of Central City. And, of course, familiarity breeds contempt. At least, everyone who is familiar with me is pretty contemptuous. The citizens began losing a little of their awe of me. That's when the complaints started.

They complained that I didn't act the way super heroes were expected to act. They pointed out, for example, that I didn't keep my true identity secret. I didn't keep changing from one persona to the other all the time. I didn't understand the point of constantly changing back and forth from mild mannered Frank Burly to bad mannered Flying Detective all day long. I mean, what's the damned point? So I wore my costume everywhere I went. People would give me strange looks when I was sitting in a coffee shop, with my jet pack on idle, having some eggs. They seemed to think I should go back home and change just to have lunch. Screw that.

Since my identity wasn't a secret, people around me became targets. Criminals seemed to think they could stop my interference in their affairs by kidnapping my friends. I told them they weren't very close friends anyway, just kill them. They called my bluff and killed one, but I didn't care, so they let the rest go. I didn't care about that either.

Each day there were more complaints about the way I did my job. People were focusing more on my failures than on my successes now. They complained about the innocent people I had hurt, the stolen money that was found in my costume, and that little crippled girl I was supposed to take on a goodwill flight around the world. Hey, I forget where I dropped her, okay?

Still, despite all the complaints, the citizens of Central City had to admit I was doing my main job, which was to stop the raids on the industrial district. There hadn't been a raid since I started.

Then the super villain Napoleon struck again,

damn him. Another major raid was launched on the city. The biggest one so far.

The Mayor was delighted. Now the city would get some real value for its money. He shined the Flying Detective Signal up in the sky and happily waited for me to come stop the raid, as per our agreement

He had to wait awhile.

When I saw the signal in the sky, I admit I hesitated. While I was more than happy to accept $1,500 a week to protect the city, I was kind of hoping that I wouldn't really have to.

The city thought of me as their insurance policy, and that's kind of the way I looked at it too. I was there to give them a feeling of security—and you can't put a price on that feeling—and then when the time came to pay off, I would find a way to weasel out of it, just like an insurance company. The last thing I wanted to do was to actually try to capture an army of inhuman monsters, commanded by some nut case who thought he was Napoleon. A guy could get hurt doing stuff like that.

But now that the time had come, I couldn't think of a single way to weasel out of my obligations. I guess that's why insurance companies get the big bucks. They can think on their feet. I can't.

As I watched the smiling outline of me flashing insistently in the sky, I realized I was in a bind. If I didn't at least make a token appearance during this crisis, I could pretty much kiss my $1,500 a week goodbye. That, I decided, was out of the question. So I climbed out from under my bed, fired up my jet pack and soared out over the city, heading for the industrial district.

A great cheer went up when I arrived at the scene of the raid. The streets were lined with people happily waving pennants with my name on them, and holding up their children so they could see me in action and watch the guts fly.

I took one look at the size of the army I was expected to kick the living shit out of, and realized I had no chance. There were at least two thousand of the mechanical creatures looting the buildings, and another five hundred or so standing guard. Those guards were now looking my way, and beginning to advance towards me.

There was only one thing to do, and I did it. Suddenly roaring back up into the sky, with a hearty "Up, Down, and Away!" I flew off to save myself, leaving the city to its fate.

CHAPTER FOUR

Twenty minutes later, the Mayor and Commissioner Brenner were walking the streets looking for me. They were, apparently, determined to get their money's worth out of me. When they got to a line of dumpsters near my office, they started looking in those. Why do people always look for me in garbage cans? I mean, how do they know?

They opened the first dumpster in the line and immediately the last dumpster blasted open and The Flying Detective roared out and spun through the sky.

By the time I could orient myself, I found that I was spinning back towards the industrial district. I didn't like that. I didn't like any of this. I had been hoping that I could just lay low in a nice garbage can somewhere until this whole thing blew over, then show up for work tomorrow morning and play dumb about the whole thing. What robbery? What cowardice? Where's my check? That sort of thing.

Once I managed to straighten myself out in

the sky, I looked down and saw that I was right over the scene of the robbery, which was still in progress. And I saw that the creatures down there had seen me. That didn't alarm me too much. There was no way I was going to go down to where they were. They could stand there until they were fifty and we still wouldn't be any closer to each other. Then I saw about twenty of the newer shinier looking creatures suddenly roar up into the sky, jet exhaust coming out of their rear ends. Obviously something new had been added. Something I didn't like one bit.

I frantically tried to turn in about five directions at once, and somehow managed to throw something out of whack on my jet pack. Suddenly I didn't have any control over the machine at all. I began making high speed figure eights in the sky, along with barrel rolls, wing-overs, reverse Cuban eights, corkscrew rolls, outside loops, stall turns, and flat spins. You name a way of being out of control in an aircraft and I performed that maneuver. At one point I was actually hopping across the sky like a grasshopper. I looked like the greatest trick flyer in the world.

The creatures tried to stay with me, doing their best to match me harebrained stunt for harebrained stunt, all the while firing some kind of laser beams at me from their eyes. But their obviously superior equipment and flying skills were no match for my accidental acrobatics.

One by one my pursuers came to grief. They would be corkscrewing right behind me as I went between two buildings, and when I came out, after performing four high speed right turns and an Immelman, I was alone. Every time one of them got on my tail, I would end up miraculously surviving and he would end up with his picture on the wall of some bar in the high desert.

Within ten minutes, I was alone in the sky, clinging to the ledge of the Central City Bank Building, my jet pack roaring, with no way to get down. All of my directional controls were gone now. It's like the whole machine was stuck in neutral.

I clung to the ledge, calmly running through a mental checklist of all of the things I... then lost my grip mid-list and plummeted to the ground, my jet pack still going full blast. I hit the street and exploded, taking out one of the robbers' getaway trucks and scattering unconscious creatures in all directions.

I was hurt, but not as hurt as I would have been if I wasn't used to it. As I slowly got to my feet, people rushed up to congratulate me. Never had any of them seen flying like that before. And, though I hadn't foiled the entire robbery, I had at least stopped one of the trucks. And I had killed or captured twenty nine of the creatures. I was the hero of the day.

I went triumphantly along to the police station with my captured robbers, giving them a little push when I felt they weren't moving fast enough, and accepting congratulations from all sides for the great job I did, and for being such a helluva guy.

The police had problems booking my captives because, for one thing, they didn't have any fingerprints. And their faces were all the same. How do you book guys like that? How do you arrange them in a line-up? Modern police methods require different faces. The police thought everybody knew that. These robbers made them mad.

The creatures didn't have hearts or other internal organs either. What they did have was a variety of propulsion mechanisms—electric motors, clockwork, steam power, storage batteries and so on. They were also equipped with built-in radio control receivers and rudimentary mechanical brains. I asked the police if they always cut open people they arrested like this, and they asked if this was off the record, and I said it wasn't, so they didn't say any more.

I tagged along as my prisoners were taken down to the holding cells. On the way, I noticed they were all wearing neat shiny black rings on their fingers. I asked about these rings. What did they signify? One of them cleared his mechanical throat and said in a mechanical voice that the rings had to do with a club they were all in. I asked if I could join this club, because it sounded like fun, and sometimes I get lonely, but he said no.

Everyone was delighted by my heroic defense of the city—Mayor Safeton most of all. This was exactly what he had hoped would happen when he had hired me. This was the kind of thing that gets politicians votes they don't deserve. He asked an aide if there was any chance they could get the election moved up to tomorrow. The aide said he'd look into it.

I was asked to make dozens of public appearances and speeches over the next few weeks. I was glad to do this because it made me feel like a big-shot, and there's no better feeling than that, scientists say, but unfortunately, I still wasn't very good at making speeches.

My first speech was in front of a women's group—The Pompous Asses For Values—and it didn't go over too well. My speech was too brief, for one thing, lasting only a couple of minutes before I ran out of material and started to stare. And the question and answer session afterwards got kind of dicey.

"What moral message do you feel you are sending to the youth of this city?" asked a pompous ass in the third row.

I scratched my head. "Shit, lady, I dunno."

Everyone got all upset when I said this. I looked around at all the aged angry faces. "What the shit is the problem now?"

Instead of answering me, they just got more upset. I felt I was losing control of the situation. I made an excuse and left early. "I've got to take a shit," I told them.

After a few more speeches—to groups as varied as The Pompous Asses For Freedom, their great rivals The Pompous Asses For Liberty, The Pompous Asses For Progress, and The Pompous Asses For Change—I started to get the hang of public speaking. I learned not to say anything except what they wanted to hear, like how important their group was, and how right they were about everything. I learned to make long speeches instead of short ones, so there wouldn't be time for questions afterwards. And I learned not to say "shit" so much. Or so loud.

While I was making all these appearances, there were four more robbery attempts on Central City's industrial district by the "Napoleon of Crime," as the papers had cleverly begun to call him, and I'm proud to say I partially foiled them all. Twice I fell out of the sky onto some of the raiders when I was trying to leave town carrying too heavy of a suitcase. Once I blew up when I was approaching them with a flag of truce and the plans for a nearby fort. And once my jet exhaust caused a fire that burned down the part of the city they were attempting to rob. They had to just turn around and go back where they came from, empty-handed. All of these skirmishes were considered great victories by the people of Central City. They were glad to be able to cheer about anything at this point.

I was enjoying my new found celebrity, and my bank account was bulging with all the speaking fees I had been getting, not to mention my hefty weekly salary. And the value of my autograph had gone up to $180 now. I thought my life couldn't get any better. Unfortunately, I was right. My life suddenly got much worse.

I had just gotten home one night after serving as Grand Marshal of the Pompous Ass Parade, when there was a metallic knock on my door.

When I answered it, I found a creature standing there with a note. The note was unsigned, but the writer said that if I kept meddling in his affairs, and didn't drop the whole Flying Detective thing right now, the next raid wouldn't be against Central City. It would be against me. The last five pages of the note were just graphic descriptions of what was going to happen to me if I didn't heed this warning. It wasn't pleasant reading. It almost made me sick.

I asked the creature who the message was from. Did Napoleon write this? But he didn't reply. He was waiting for me to sign a piece of paper indicating I had received the message, and for any tip I might feel he had earned. As I signed the receipt, and stiffed him as far as the tip was concerned, I noticed there was a faint whirring noise coming from him.

"You should see a doctor about that whirring noise," I advised.

He looked a little alarmed, then defiant. He took the receipt book I had signed, pocketed his pen and walked quickly away, the propeller on his ass whirring even louder.

In a case of unfortunate timing, the next day was the day I was to be given the Key to the City for my unstinting efforts to protect life and property in Central City. I would have preferred to have made my announcement at some other time, when there weren't so many smiling faces looking up at me, but it had to be done now. I don't believe in ignoring warnings from super villains. It isn't healthy.

So, after they had given me the Key, and I had made a long rambling self-congratulatory acceptance speech, I announced my retirement. The Flying Detective, I told them, was no more.

"My job here is done," I told the stunned audience. "Up, Down, Away, and Goodbye."

As I was leaving the podium, they took back the Key To The City I had just been given. I was disappointed about that. I figured it would have opened some doors for me. Not professionally, you understand. Just some doors.

CHAPTER FIVE

So my career as The Flying Detective was over. And it was only Chapter Five. It was with a trace of sadness that I packed away my costume, my extra pairs of underwear, and my junior grappling hooks. They were useless now, except for whatever historical importance they might have.

I didn't put away my jet pack. I still wanted to use that for occasional flights down to the post office to mail letters, or for quick trips to the bathroom. It beats walking.

It was while I was packing these things away that the Mayor and Police Commissioner Brenner stormed into my office.

"I can't believe what I've heard," said the Mayor. "You're quitting? I can't believe I heard that."

"You want to hear it again?"

"No."

The Commissioner eyed me bleakly. "Why are you quitting?"

I showed them the threatening message I had

received, and held my hand up in the air to show how big the creature was who had delivered it.

"But you've got super powers!" protested the Mayor. "Nothing can harm you. You said so yourself when we hired you." He crumpled up the threatening message and threw it in the wastebasket. "Now get back to work."

I was about to tell him that I didn't really have super powers, that I'd been playing them for suckers all this time, and that every one of those bullets that had been fired into me had really hurt, but I changed my mind at the last moment. Telling the truth, though the right thing to do, kids, has never worked out too well for me. I figured I'd better stick with lying on this one.

"He also possesses super powers and abilities," I informed them somberly. "Powers even greater than my own. I cannot defeat him. So get yourself another boy. I quit."

Important people don't like taking "no" for an answer. That's how you can tell they're important. The two men stamped around my office for nearly an hour, yelling at me. They said they'd sue me, jail me, denounce me, disgrace me, even revoke my P.I. license and throw it in my super face. I said that was better than killing me, which is what the super villain was going to do. I said if they couldn't top killing me, they were wasting their breath. Finally they gave up and left, shouting threats back over their shoulders at me all the way to the elevator.

I didn't worry too much about them making a big public stink about my retirement. After all, they had hired me, giving me a great deal of the taxpayer's money, and taking a 10% "agent's fee" for themselves under the table. That wasn't the sort of thing you wanted to splash all over the newspapers. That was the sort of thing you wanted to sweep under the rug and put a chair on it. And sweep they did. I didn't hear any more squawks from City Hall about my quitting. I didn't get my last paycheck, they hung on to that, but I chalked that up to experience and forgot about it.

The problem was, none of the citizenry believed The Flying Detective had retired. Super heroes didn't retire. They fought the forces of evil until they triumphed. Oh, sure, they could be put out of commission temporarily by being injured, or weakened by some rare alien metal, or imprisoned in a different dimension by the Evil Doctor Somebody, or sent off on a wild goose chase by The Wise-Cracker, or something like that. The public could lose the use of them in that way. But super heroes couldn't just quit. That never happened. Not in any comic book. The public wasn't falling for that.

The media treated the whole thing like it was a joke. The greatest crime fighter in the history of Central City retire? Don't make the media laugh. It was obviously a ruse of some kind. They knew I must have something up my sleeve, and they knew if they talked to each other long enough they'd find out what it was.

All this, of course, made me more than a little uncomfortable. I was retired. Out of the business for good. And I wanted everyone, but especially that one person, to know it.

I made it a point, whenever I encountered a person in trouble, to leave them that way, or if possible, get them into more trouble. If I saw a bank being robbed, I crossed to the other side of the street and pulled my hat down farther over my eyes. If I saw a cop chasing a criminal, I would tackle that cop. And if a dog showed up with some story about somebody being trapped in a mine or something, I would pretend not to understand him.

I stopped signing 8X10 photographs of The Flying Detective when they were handed to me by fans. I offered to sign 8X10s of me in my Frank Burly detective outfit, a nice shot of me looking the other way in a crisis, or a moodily lit 5X7 of me letting everybody down, but nobody wanted those pictures.

This approach gradually began to show results. The smiles that greeted me when I walked down the street were turning to sneers. The cheers to snorts. The requests for autographs to requests that I get out of the way and let the decent people through.

Then disaster struck. I saved the damned city again.

Napoleon had launched another one of his raids on the industrial district. This one was the biggest one yet. Entire warehouses were being loaded onto giant getaway trucks. The police had been slapped aside with even more ease than usual, and were already on their way to their session with the police psychiatrists. The citizens were in a state of panic.

Immediately my phone started ringing and people started banging on my door, saying I should come out and save them because I was their only hope, and they didn't mean the things they said about me before. But I didn't hear them because I was already at 14,000 feet and climbing, with a suitcase in either hand, heading for a different state. This was something I just didn't want to get involved in.

I guess I shouldn't have tried to get out of town so fast. I had so many booster rockets on my back there was no way to balance them right for level flight. You're probably wondering whether that's important or not. Well, I'm here to tell you it is.

The raiders had just finished packing the last of the city's polyvinylchloride and model airplane glue into their getaway trucks and were about to leave, when a distant screaming sound made them look up. I was pinwheeling across the sky, shooting out sparks like a one-man Fourth of July celebration. Suddenly I exploded in a shower of sparks, jet fuel, speedometers and swastikas, high above them, and plummeted screaming to earth onto their leader.

As the dismayed and suddenly leaderless creatures beat a hasty retreat, the crowd rushed up to congratulate me.

I struggled, cursing, to my feet, amidst handshakes and claps on the back, and looked around for my suitcases. I had to get out of here.

Or did I? Suddenly I noticed that the super

villain who had been scaring me half to death all this time was lying on the street, unconscious, with my foot in his mouth.

As thrilled citizens crowded around me and flashbulbs went off in my face, catching and preserving for future generations my every blink and twitch, the Mayor rushed up, put one of his feet in Napoleon's mouth also, and pumped my hand.

"Wonderful! Wonderful, my boy! You, that is to say 'we,' have done it! We're heroes!"

We posed for more pictures, this time with our feet on Napoleon's eyes. The crowd cheered. Hey, I thought, this is working out all right.

Unfortunately, all was not as it seemed. Just after I had finished telling a group of awestruck reporters all about how I had faked my own retirement and lured the super villain to his Waterloo, ha ha, word came that the police had examined the body of Napoleon and found that he wasn't unconscious, as everyone had thought. He wasn't dead either. He was plastic.

His body was found to contain the same radio control receivers the other creatures had, though his were a little bigger and slightly more advanced. So he wasn't the super villain after all. Someone else was. And I had probably just made that someone else very angry.

I had.

The next week was, for me, a nonstop series of assassination attempts. The super villain, whoever he really was, stopped raiding Central City entirely, and began expending all his energy in a single minded effort to blot me out of existence. He threw everything he had at me.

There were car bombs, letter bombs, all kinds of bombs. Practically everything I touched blew up. Riflemen fired at me from rooftops, alley-ways, even from Presidential motorcades. Everywhere I went I was confronted with specially designed creatures sent to assassinate me. Super thin assassins would slither under my bedroom door when I was asleep. Sugar coated assassins would somehow get into the box of cereal I was about to have for breakfast. The super villain even got the weather to turn against me. Lightning strikes followed me wherever I went, and tornados hung around outside of my office all day waiting for me to come out.

I managed to survive each assassination attempt, more or less, you know me, but I felt that one of them was bound to get me eventually. An odds-maker I knew said that mathematically I had to have been killed at least eight times already. He was willing to bet me $500 I was already dead. I figured I'd better do something. Quick.

I took out an ad in the paper with an open letter to the super villain, explaining that there was no need for him to expend all this energy assassinating me because I wasn't in the super hero business anymore. I had quit. I was sorry for any inconvenience I had caused him in the past, and I wished him nothing but success in all his future criminal endeavors. I added that I hoped his family was well, and wished him a very merry Christmas.

Either he didn't believe what I had written in my letter, or he hadn't seen it. I probably should have bought a full page ad, now that I think about it.

I finally decided that the only chance I had of convincing the super villain that I was no threat to him, was to meet him face to face and talk to him. And maybe kill him.

CHAPTER SIX

The skies over Central City were full of flying creatures out looking for me, so I had to be careful when I began my search for the super villain. I couldn't use my jet pack. I wouldn't last five seconds up there. I had out-flown the creatures the first time, but there were more of them now. And you can't always count on going out of control when you need to. Plus, I felt it might send the wrong message. The story was, The Flying Detective was retired. So I set out on foot, keeping to back-alleys as much as possible.

I began asking around at the scenes of recent robberies, to see if any of the residents had spotted any suspicious-looking super criminals hanging around the area.

Most people don't notice things like that, they don't notice much of anything, I'm surprised they've lived so long, but one old lady said she'd seen someone suspicious hanging around all right. She'd seen him good. I pressed her for details. She turned out to be a more observant witness than I usually run into. Most of the people

I question usually say things like: "He was tall and short." Inadequate descriptions like that. But this lady was very observant.

"He was six feet tall," she informed me, "182 pounds, wearing a brown coat, checkered socks, and blue boxer shorts."

"You're very observant, Miss..."

"Hemple. I would have seen more but it was dark. And he knocked me down when I tried to get his underpants off."

"And you only saw him that one time?"

"Yes. He doesn't come down this block anymore. He goes around it."

So I had one lead already. But I wasn't sure I was going to bother to follow up on it. It didn't sound like the guy with the blue underwear was the guy I was looking for. Super villains don't usually let themselves be manhandled and stripped by old women like that. It was nice to know somebody else wears underwear like mine though.

I spent the rest of the afternoon checking around in one of the rougher areas of the industrial district, to see if I could turn up anything useful there. I ended up learning a lot: I learned that I should mind my own business, that I was asking for it, that I didn't seem to be getting the message, that if I didn't think they meant it I was sorely mistaken, and that the same thing would happen to me again if I ever came back. It wasn't the kind of information I was looking for exactly, but at least I hadn't wasted my day entirely. I'd picked up some useful tips. Tips about me.

Then a crook who owed me a favor—it was my confused testimony on the stand that had saved him from the chair and gotten him elected Lt. Governor—told me that I should check out a certain unlisted building on the South Side. He wouldn't tell me any more than that. Just said I should check it out. Then he went back to ripping off the public and vomiting on our freedoms, like he had been elected to do.

When I got to the mysterious building he had mentioned, I found all the rooms and offices locked and apparently empty, until I got to the penthouse. There was sinister music coming from inside, so I opened the door and walked in.

I was immediately intercepted by a white haired impeccably dressed old gentleman.

"Good afternoon, sir," he said. "May I have today's password, please?"

"I don't think I know today's password," I replied. "Yesterday's either."

He nodded amiably as if I had said the right thing, but began loading a small silver pistol. "I'd have a stab at it, if I were you, sir."

"Shoehorn."

"Very good, sir. Come right in."

I tried not to look as surprised as I was. I followed him into the room.

"You don't have to keep saying 'shoehorn,' sir," he told me as he hung up my coat. "Once is sufficient."

The main room was like one of those

Gentlemen's Clubs you read about in long novels. High backed chairs, thick rugs, antique weapons and sporting prints on the walls, small discrete signs that said "No Loud Talking" and "No Pepper," and so on. All very traditional.

What was untraditional about this particular club was its members. The snatches of conversation I heard as I walked through the room told me exactly where I was.

"Where young super villains go wrong," one was saying, "is they kill everybody. You've got to leave somebody alive to pay you."

Another was reliving an old battle from his past. "An entire army against me and all I had was my weather machine and my lust for gold."

"What did you do?"

"I kicked their ass, that's what I did."

"Gosh!"

"You've fallen into my trap!" giggled one of the younger members, as he wrestled with his neighbor.

"No, no, you've fallen into my trap!"

Another had a handful of maps and charts he was showing to the man next to him. "So after I make it snow, you make time stop moving."

"Gotcha."

"With everybody stopped and wet, we can make our move."

"Oh boy!"

They were all super villains. I was in the Super Villain Club.

I made the rounds, shaking hands with the various members and telling them "shoehorn."

They asked if I was a new super villain in town, as they had not seen me around before. I said I was new to the club, but not to the business. I had conquered the planet once already, when I was younger. That raised me in their estimation. Not many of them had done that.

I sat down next to one of the older members, who was snoozing in a leather chair by the fire. His legs were moving, as if he were dreaming he was running away from good people. I coughed discretely to attract his attention, which unfortunately set off a fit of severe coughing that made all of my guns fall out of my pockets. This attracted everyone else's attention except his, so I moved away to talk to someone else.

I saw what appeared to be the Devil sitting in the corner of the room looking bored and flipping souls into a hat. They made an "oh woe!" sound as they flew through the air. I went up to him.

"Devil, eh?" I said, a little uneasily. "Do I get three wishes now? I forget how it works."

"You've got me confused with someone else."

I nodded. "I do that a lot." I watched him flip a few more souls into the hat.

He lit a cigarette with his breath and looked me over as he puffed.

"You're a detective, aren't you?"

I couldn't admit that, of course. I was here incognito. "Yes, I'm a detective," I heard myself saying. "And a rotten one I am, too."

"How would you like to be the greatest detective in the world? To be able to solve the most complicated crime in seconds, run like the wind, and shoot like Aaron Burr? Would you like that, Frank?"

"Hell, yes. Wait a minute, though. Is there some catch?"

"You would be required to do some small services for me—talking people into being bad, badmouthing organized religion, collecting a few stray souls for me—just small things. The rest we can discuss after you're dead."

"Now you really sound like the Devil."

"Sounding like the Devil is not the same as being the Devil. Not in this state, anyway. Read the law books if you don't believe me. I'm just an ordinary super villain, like everyone else. I am not the Devil."

"Oh no, of course not," I said. "Anybody can make me run faster."

I thanked him for the offer, but said I guessed I'd pass on it for now. He shrugged, lit another cigarette, and opened his pocketbook to examine the wailing moth-like creatures he had in there. I recognized one of them. It was my Uncle Phil.

"Hi, Uncle Phil."

"Hello, Frank. Would you like to make a nickel? Get your Uncle Phillip out of here and he'll give you a shiny new nickel."

I turned to the Devil. "Does he have any money in there? Nickels or anything?"

"No."

That settled that. I continued around the room talking with the various super villains, always making it sound like I was a new member who was just making conversation.

"Have you been trying to kill me?" I would ask, casually. "I'm just curious. Or we could talk about the weather, if you like. The weather's been trying to kill me too. Is that your doing? My name's Frank, by the way."

All of them denied being the man I was looking for, but suggested it might be one of the other members: Professor Kryptonite over there, or Colonel Awful, perhaps.

I excitedly checked out each new lead, but kept coming up empty. Finally, when I started being pointed back to the same people I'd already talked to, I gave it up and started to leave.

The aged doorkeeper helped me on with my coat and said he couldn't help overhearing the question I'd been asking, since I had asked it so many times and with such growing anger, and he hoped I wouldn't mind him taking the liberty of sticking in his two cents, but the person I was looking for might be Overkill.

"Who?"

"Professor Overkill."

I looked back into the room. "Which one is he?"

The doorman shook his head ruefully and explained that Overkill wasn't a member of the club. He had been denied membership on numerous occasions.

"The members don't agree with his methods, sir. They feel he tends to overdo things. They feel his work is too broad. So his many applications have been rejected."

I asked where I might find this Overkill,

pressing some money into his aged hand to help him remember.

"His application forms state his residence as Revenge Island, sir," he said, throwing the quarter away. "That's right out in the middle of the lake. The island that appears to be frowning."

I thanked him and asked if there was a special word I had to say to get out of there. He said there wasn't, so I left.

I spent the next few days trying to get to Revenge Island. It was easy to find. It was the only angry looking island in the lake. But it was impossible to get to.

There were no boats for hire, so I tried swimming there, but remembered after I had gone 50 feet, straight down, and had been lying face down on the bottom for awhile, that I couldn't swim.

My jet pack could have gotten me to the island easily enough, of course, but I couldn't approach the super villain that way. It would look like The Flying Detective was coming to get him and wring his filthy neck. That was the last thing I wanted him to think. So that was out.

I tried chartering a plane, but apparently the super villain was one step ahead of me. Once the plane got up in the air, it started buffeting around violently and then went into a dive. I worked my way forward to the cockpit. The pilot was gone. I couldn't figure out the controls, didn't even know where to start, so I went back to my seat and read a magazine until the plane crashed.

After doctors took the casts off my legs, and

worked the tubes out of my nose, and hammered my rear end back into shape, I tried mailing myself to the island in a package. I had a buddy who worked down at the post office help me with the operation. But I wouldn't pop for first class postage, so I had to go junk mail. I got to the island before the end of the month, but they tossed me out unopened. I was in a garbage can for almost a week before a truck picked me up.

All these attempts were made more difficult because I had to constantly keep my eye out for the super villain's minions. They were still out looking for me, as determinedly as before, but, to my relief, there had recently been a change in tactics. Now they weren't trying to kill me, they were just trying to capture me. I guess once you've tried to kill somebody 138 times and he's still not dead, it's time to try something else.

So now all the time I was trying to find a way onto the island, I had to avoid a series of clever Rube Goldbergian traps. Remember that game "Mouse Trap"? It's like I was living in one of those. The Deluxe Version. I'd start to open a door, for example, and the minute I turned the knob, the door would swing up and everything around me would start moving, and baskets would start being lowered onto me to trap me. I'd have to drop the cheese and make a run for it.

Fortunately, the traps were all a little too clever. They seemed to be designed to trap a mastermind. I wasn't a mastermind. I just wanted that piece of cheese. So they didn't work on me.

Then it suddenly occurred to me that maybe I

shouldn't be trying so hard to avoid the people who were trying to capture me and take me to where I wanted to go. That didn't make much sense, when I thought about it. If I would just let them capture me, it would help everybody out. We could all stop working so hard.

I tied myself up in a gunny sack, and left me in the middle of the street. Nothing happened, so I wrote "Burly" on the sack and got back in.

After a couple of days, the super villain's creatures spotted me. They walked up to the sack, read what it said, looked at each other, shrugged, then picked me up. I offered no resistance.

They began carrying me off, but I weigh more than I look, so they ended up, as so many people do, dragging me. They took me on a long, circuitous journey. I don't think I've ever said "Are we there yet?" so many times in my life. Eventually we got to a high cliff face. They began to climb, pulling me along behind them on a rope.

"What happens if we fall?" I asked, nervously.

"What do you think happens?"

"I'd rather hear it from you."

"Quiet in the sack," said the leader.

I'd swear that during our journey we went up that same cliff at least twice more. But I can't be sure. I tried to leave a trail of bread crumbs, but the crumbs just stayed in the sack with me.

Finally we ended up at the 1st Avenue Pier, which isn't very far from where they had originally picked me up.

While we were waiting for the launch from the island to come get us, I asked why we had spent all that time going up all those cliffs and jumping over those secret chasms. Why hadn't we just taken the bus here like I always did? They said because they don't do things that way, that's why.

When we got to the island, my captors dragged me off the boat, across a couple acres of lawn, up and down a flight of stone steps a few times, then emptied me out into a dungeon.

"How long do I have to stay here?"

"Forever."

"No, seriously, how long are we talking about?"

They didn't answer.

CHAPTER SEVEN

I demanded to see the super villain who owned the island. I insisted that I be taken to him immediately.

"You're not running this dungeon," said one of the guards.

"Wait a minute, Bob," said one of the other guards, as the first guard was slapping me silly. "Maybe we better check."

They went away and came back fifteen minutes later. "You're not running this dungeon," they said, and resumed slapping me.

Between slaps, I told them that I really needed to talk to their master. It was important. They explained to me that Mr. Overkill didn't talk to prisoners. He had more interesting people to talk to. Guards, for example.

"But I have important information for him," I explained.

"I'll give it to him," said one of the guards, coming forward and holding out his hand.

"I need to give it to him personally. It's in my head."

"Jeff, get a knife. Something in this guy's head."

I suddenly didn't like where this was going. "Uh... wait a minute. I've forgotten it now."

Jeff stopped in front of me, holding the knife. He frowned. "Nothing in your head?"

"No."

He shrugged and put his knife away.

I decided I needed to get the guards on my side somehow. Sometimes money does the trick. I asked one of them how much he was making.

"$12.50 an hour," he replied.

I thought about this, then shook my head. "Well, I can't pay you that much. That's ridiculous. How about $7.00 an hour?" Then I added: "For three hours."

This didn't sound all that good to him. He was having a hard time making ends meet on what he was getting, especially since he had to buy his own keys. I wouldn't raise my offer, so we didn't have a deal. The guards left, locking the door behind them. So there went that idea.

I sat down with my back against a wall and pondered my situation. It wasn't perfect, being imprisoned forever never is, but at least I was on the island.

After I'd been sitting there for about an hour, I noticed there were about a dozen guys in the dungeon with me. It was their loud discussion about how unobservant and ugly I was that finally attracted my attention to them. I took one look at them and was amazed. I was locked up with the most famous detectives in the world.

There was Phillip Manley, the two-fisted film noir detective, who had spent his celebrated career getting beaten up nearly as much as I did. We rubbed our eyes when we saw each other.

Then there was Sherringford Harper, the famous British amateur sleuth. He could tell you your whole life story just by watching you go by in a train. He was like Sherlock Holmes, except without all the trademarks. Anybody could write about him. That's what I liked about him.

The others in the dungeon were equally celebrated. Among them were: the fattest detective in the world, the thinnest detective, the loudest, and the farthest (he always stood in the back of any room). A lot of them were heroes of mine, who had failed to send me autographed 8X10s when I wrote and asked for them, so I admit I was a little glad they were trapped in here. Serves them right, I thought. On the other hand, hey, I'm in here too.

I asked them what they were all doing here, and they said they had each been on the trail of the dreaded super villain Overkill. But he had bested them one by one.

"He's a devil, that one," said the thin detective.

I said I might have met him then, and described my experience at the Super Villain Club. But they said that was probably just the real Devil I met.

"How did he capture you?" asked Harper. "I'll bet it was something damned devilish."

"He picked up the sack I was in."

They were a little disappointed by this, at first. "Well, that's pretty devilish," said one, finally.

"Devilishly simple, I call it," said another.

As clever as he was, they still felt they would get the best of Overkill eventually. But they would have to get out of here first. For this, they had a plan. Actually they had twelve plans, each starring the detective who had thought of it, with the others playing demeaning subordinate roles, often with burnt cork on their faces. No plan had received more than one vote, so they decided to try them all, starting with Harper's.

He approached me to sound me out on the subject. As the others watched the door for any sign of approaching guards, he knelt down next to me and spoke in a low whisper.

"The safety, indeed the whole future of the world, depends on what you do next."

I tried not to fart, but it was no use.

When we could hear again, he resumed: "What you do next, is..."

After our ears had stopped ringing and dogs in the next county had stopped barking from what must have been the biggest fart of my career, he tried once more, using a different setup line.

"Listen," he said.

As I farted along, he began outlining their elaborate escape plan, but I stopped him before he'd gotten very far. I wasn't interested in getting off the island. I had gone to a lot of trouble to get onto this island. I wasn't going to leave until I'd talked to Overkill. So they could escape if they wanted to, but it would have to be without me.

"Even if you do get out of this dungeon, how are you going to get off the island?" I asked.

Harper said they had spent the last three months constructing a small sea-going vessel using the only materials available to them.

I looked around the dungeon. "You made a boat out of ants?"

He hesitated, then said: "Yes." He saw my look and bristled slightly. "Ants float, Mr. Burly. They float beautifully."

I shrugged and said I wished them luck, but they could count me out. Harper stared at me for a long moment, then nodded grimly and went back to the others. I had a feeling I'd probably never get that autographed 8X10 now.

I woke up the next morning to find that I was alone in the cell. The other detectives had apparently escaped during the night. I saw my chance to get in good with Overkill.

"Guards!" I hollered. "The bad prisoners have escaped! The good prisoner is still here!"

The dungeon door flew open and the guards rushed in. They frantically looked around the dungeon, then rounded on me.

"What do you mean by frightening us like that?" one of them demanded. "No one has escaped." He pointed at a drawing on the wall of twelve detectives, waving. "The prisoners are right there!"

Well I don't know where the phrase "As smart as a guard" came from, but it wasn't coined to describe these particular guards. It took me twenty minutes to convince them that the real prisoners had escaped, which I finally did by erasing one of the detectives. You should have seen the guards' jaws drop when I did that. That's the first time I ever saw actual exclamation points and question marks appear above somebody's head. (In case you're interested, I felt one of the marks and they're made of hair.)

One reason it was so hard to get the guards to believe there had been an escape was because they knew it was impossible. The only way to escape from this dungeon was if the guards stupidly left the door open. Which they had, of course, when they ran in. And the door had remained open for twenty minutes while they argued with me about who was still here and who wasn't. It was at some point during this argument, I found out later, that the detectives had rushed out of the dark corner they had been hiding in and ran through the open door to freedom, carrying their ant-boat.

I told the stunned guards to inform Overkill that the escaped prisoners were probably somewhere out on the lake. There might still be time to catch them. And I recommended that he bring some ant spray.

Within an hour the detectives had been caught and returned to captivity. They had made it to about halfway across the lake before seagulls started eating their boat. The super villain's security force had re-captured them just before they sank.

"Thanks, Burly," said Manley, as the detectives were brought back to the dungeon.

"You are quite welcome."

"I was being sarcastic."

"Uh... oh, yeah... so was I."

The head guard arrived and glared at the detectives. "So! You try to make me look bad, eh?" He turned to one of the other guards. "Put these guys in an even worse dungeon."

"But, boss..."

"Do it." He turned to me. "You, come with me."

To my amazement he led me through the cell door, up the stairs, and across the lawn towards the huge fortress in the center of the island.

"Where are you taking me?"

"Dinner."

CHAPTER EIGHT

"Welcome, Mr. Burly! Welcome! At last we meet. Sit down and have some wine. Dinner will be served shortly."

I sat down at the end of a long table and looked at my host, the dangerous super villain Overkill. He was considerably smaller in real life than he was in my imagination. Instead of being forty feet high with jackhammers for fingers, he was about five foot four, with standard fingers. He was fiftyish and somewhat pudgy. He didn't seem all that dangerous up close.

I noticed he was studying me as carefully as I was studying him. I also noticed he had a large gun on the table next to his wine glass. The guards had their guns out too. And there were framed guns on the wall, cocked and pointed at me. This guy wasn't taking any chances.

Nobody had said anything for awhile, so I thought it advisable to make some small talk.

"I hear they won't let you in the Super Villain Club."

His face twisted horribly. He grabbed the top

of his head and began shouting: "Kill Maim Frighten Destroy!"

He began smashing plates and glasses, tipped over a nearby serving cart, then pulled up a large stretch of carpet. Then he seemed to get hold of himself. He coughed self consciously.

"Yes, well, I didn't really want to be a member anyway. Bunch of nonsense, kill destroy. Now, Mr. Burly, I wanted to meet you, because I'm intrigued by your recent actions. Not only did you not take part in the escape attempt by the other prisoners, you actually helped foil it. Why?"

"I wanted to talk to you. I hoped you would see me if I helped you out."

"Very well. I've seen you. What's on your mind?"

I explained that for quite some time now he had been getting entirely the wrong impression about me. That I was out to foil his plans or something. Few things could be farther from the truth. Or further from the truth, I wasn't sure which. Overkill didn't know which one it was either. We decided it didn't matter. I said that though I had originally been hired to stop him, I was now happily retired. So there was no need for him to view me as an enemy. I wouldn't harm a fly. I wasn't the enemy of a fly.

"I find this difficult to believe, Mr. Flying Detective. You broke up one of my robberies just last week. You captured one of my generals. I have a picture of you with your foot in his mouth."

I said it was an accident. In fact, all of the robberies I'd ever broken up were accidents. I was never trying to foil any crimes at all. I was just trying to screw the city out of $1,500 a week. I explained my insurance company metaphor to him.

He studied me for awhile, then picked up the large gun next to his wine glass, and replaced it with a slightly smaller gun. He was beginning to trust me.

I noticed he had a picture of me on the wall. I asked what it was for.

"Ever since you started meddling in my affairs, I've been studying your picture to try to get inside your mind, to figure out what makes you tick, so I could find a way to defeat you."

This was interesting to me. "What did the pictures tell you?"

"Well, at first they told me: 'Hey, this guy is stupid,' but I knew that couldn't be. So I got a different picture of you. A side view, of you looking at something off camera. That picture gave me a different insight. I looked at that and thought: 'Hey, this guy sees all.'"

"I'd like to get a copy of that 2nd picture."

"I'll have one sent to your dungeon."

"Thanks."

As the dinner progressed, Overkill became more and more convinced that he had been mistaken about me. The gun next to his plate kept getting smaller and smaller until finally it was replaced by a big knife.

"This is pleasant, getting together like this, don't you think?" asked Overkill.

"Very enjoyable."

"We must do this every couple of years. You'll join me for dinner, we'll talk, then, it's back in the hole."

"Count me in."

"Friends do dine with each other on occasion. And I want us to be friends."

"As do I."

"Friends do things for each other, too. I'd like to demonstrate my friendship for you, Frank. For example, do you like your guard?"

"Well, not really. He's poking me in the back with his bayonet. He's been doing it all through dinner. It's probably going to leave a mark."

Overkill turned to one of his men and pointed at my guard. "Kill him!"

The guard was struck down and quietly dragged away. Overkill looked at me. There was only one thing to say at that point and I said it: "Hey, thanks."

We went on with our dinner. The food was good, but it seemed kind of ordinary for a super villain's table. I mentioned this in my tactful way, and he looked uncomfortable.

"Yes, I suppose the food should be more exotic for a man in my position. Elephant eggs, or talking caviar or something. I'm kind of new at this—don't really know all the ins and outs yet. But don't tell anybody."

"You told somebody."

"Yes, but I don't want you to."

"That doesn't seem fair to me. I want to tell somebody."

"No."

"Oh all right. New at this, eh? How long have you been a super villain?"

"Eleven months. But what I lack in experience I make up for in perseverance, stick-to-it-iveness and get-up-and-go."

"I'm not trying to hire you. I just wanted to know."

"Eleven months."

He told me his story. He hadn't started out life as a super villain. He was a toy manufacturer. The president of the Overmyer Toy Company of Flint, Michigan. He asked if I'd heard of it. I said it was my favorite.

"Authenticity was our trademark," he said proudly. "All our toys and models were authentic down to the last detail. Our toy police cars, for example, could actually arrest people. They had that authority built in. That's the kind of thing kids want, you know. They don't want a toy. They want the real thing, just on a smaller scale. 'The Real Thing, For The Price Of A Toy,' was the slogan we had for all our toys and models. That and 'If You Truly Love Your Boy, Buy Him A True-To-Life Overmyer Toy.' I thought up the slogans as well as doing the initial designs."

"I just love those slogans. And I'll bet the initial designs were outstanding."

"It pleases me that you think so." He beamed at me.

His products had done so well, he told me, that the company had gone public and he had made several billion dollars overnight. But that windfall proved to be his undoing. Six months later when the newly installed board of directors of this now publicly controlled company met for the first time, they forced him out in favor of a younger man who could talk faster.

"So I was out at 52. Finished. I had enough money to do anything I wanted with the remainder of my life, but what I wanted to do was run my toy company. And that had been taken away from me. Kill, Maim, Frighten, Destroy!"

He paused in his story to smash his end of the table to pieces with his fists, his head changing shape with anger. After the moment had passed, he sat back down, patted his head back into close to its original shape, and looked at me.

"You were saying?" he asked.

"You were telling me your back-story."

"Oh, yes, that's right. So, anyway, I found myself sitting around the house all day, not knowing what to do with myself, and feeling kind of worthless. We are carefully programmed by society, you know, to believe that life is about work. Working for them. If you're not working for them, life has no meaning, they say. That all sounded a little too convenient for society to me. A little too pat. I rebelled against the idea. I didn't want to be a cog in a machine. I wanted to be a cog running free, doing what it wanted. Cogging around, having a good time. But I didn't know what I wanted to do.

"I tried collecting stamps. People said that was a fun and instructional way to pass the time. But once you've collected them, what do you have? Stamps! That's what no one told me."

I made a sympathetic sound. I had collected a stamp once too. Bunch of bullshit.

He smoothed out the last few bulges in his head, and continued: "I grew angry at a system that would allow a man to be shoved out of the company he had inherited from his dad, who in turn had stolen it from someone else's dad, who had built it with his own two hands, on land he had stolen from the Indians. It just didn't seem right. I looked for a way to strike back at this system, and at the same time have a few laughs."

"Good thinking."

"I bought a secret island from another secret guy and started building my 'Fortress of Revenge', as I call it."

"Great name."

"Thank you."

"You know what's great about you? Everything!"

"Don't lay it on too thick."

"Brilliant note."

"And soon I will be ready to take over the world. People say I'm mad. Say it all the time. And you know what? It's starting to make me mad."

I nodded. "I'm getting angry now too."

"After all, they said George Washington was mad!"

"Who said that?"

"They said The Four Marx Brothers were mad!"

"Well..."

"They couldn't have made all those motion pictures if they were truly mad. They would have fallen behind schedule. See what I'm saying? And now they're saying I'm mad!"

"First The Marx Brothers, now you."

"Could a madman build a beautiful secret fortress like this? Could a madman hold his breath this long? Or jump this high?"

"You're not mad. Anyone can see that. You jump too high."

"Right. And what's mad about taking over the world, anyway? Somebody has to run the world, why not me? And once I take over, think of all the good I could do with unlimited power."

"And are you going to do any good?"

He thought about this. "Well, I probably won't have time. But the opportunity for good will be there."

While we were getting to know one another, I began to notice there was something strangely familiar about some of his servants. The one who was heaping green beans and chili con carne on my plate was a dead ringer for Abraham Lincoln, right down to the hole in the back of his head. I gave my host a questioning look.

"Yes, that's Lincoln," Overkill said. "I'll explain later. Eat your cuisine before the ants get it."

I went back to my food, but before the servant left I had him give me his autograph. He signed it: "Abe Lincoln #906." Later I tried to sell this autograph through a major East Coast auction house, but they said it was a fake. Hey, I watched him sign it. With his own hand. With ink he got out of his own head. Fake, my ass.

As Overkill and I talked, we discovered we had

a lot in common—distrust of the government, bitterness about our childhoods, teenage years, and adult lives, and a shared feeling that the world had been created by God in seven days just to screw us—and I could sense that my host was beginning to take a liking towards me.

After we had finished eating, Overkill stood up. "Let me show you what I'm building here, Frank."

"Lead on, Ovie."

He took me on a tour of his fortress and the surrounding grounds. It was an amazing place. Evidence of fantastic wealth was around every corner, from the solid gold fireplaces and mink driveways, to the gazebo made of ten dollar bills. He had more Old Master paintings than the Louvre in Paris. In fact, some of the ones he had were supposed to be in the Louvre. The Louvre had been looking everyplace for them, but with no luck so far.

All of these treasures, as well as the island itself, were protected from intruders and prying eyes by a wide variety of defense mechanisms. Light could be bent by powerful machinery so no matter how close you were to the island, you couldn't see it. You would just be looking around it. So the island would effectively disappear. Overkill turned the machine on to demonstrate this feature to me but turned it back off when I kept bumping into him, for some reason. The island also could be covered, at a moment's notice, by a practically invisible glass shield. It would have been completely invisible, except there were streaks and smears and bird shit on it. Overkill said he would have that cleaned when he had time. I said good.

In the unlikely event of an attack on the island, Overkill had many powerful weapons set up to defend the place. He showed me how one of them worked.

"Let's say I don't like those condominiums on the shore there. Let's say they've been saying nasty things about me, and looking at me with their windows."

"I'm with you so far."

"Okay, now watch this."

He pressed a button on a control panel. There was a rumble of shifting machinery from deep within the island, then a blinding flash. When I could see again, I saw that the condominiums had been vaporized.

"Laser cannons," Overkill said proudly. "They can take out anything within four miles of this island."

"Neat," I said. "Now let's say you like those condominiums again."

Overkill scratched his chin, then shook his head. "No, once I don't like them, I can't start liking them again. They're gone."

I thought about this. "You'd better be careful with that thing then."

"You're probably right."

All these weapons, though very impressive, seemed to me to be a bit of an over-reaction. I asked him if he was really doing all this just because he had lost his job. Could there also be some other, more personal problem that was driving him on to this megalomania? Like most people, besides being what I actually am, I'm also a psychologist.

He considered the question for a moment, then admitted that he had just quit smoking. That might have something to do with it. "You should quit too," he advised. "The smoke gets into people's drapes."

"The hell with drapes."

He looked at me as if I were mad. I wasn't mad. I just don't like drapes.

"Besides," he continued, "I'm not a megalomaniac, I'm a master mind."

"What's the capitol of India?"

He hesitated for a moment, then said firmly: "India has no capitol."

I started to argue, but changed my mind. This guy was dangerous. I had to remember that.

"My weapons aren't just defensive, you'll be pleased to know," he continued as we resumed walking, "I've also amassed an Unholy Army."

"Good for you."

"It took awhile."

"I'll bet it did."

"It's not easy to assemble an Unholy Army. Most unholy people already have unholy jobs somewhere else. It's hard to find someone who has the evil skills, who is also between gigs. Recruiting has always been a big problem. You go to high schools and speak and maybe you'll get a few bad apples to sign up, but a big organization needs thousands. That's why modern super villains never get very far with their operations. You can't get the henchmen. That's where my business sense came in. If there's a need, and nobody's filling it, fill it yourself. Using my technical knowledge as a professional toy and model maker, I began making my own henchmen, to my own specifications."

"You're great."

"I use a variety of lightweight, strong, modeling materials: molded foam, polyvinyl chloride, balsa and other light woods, titanium for strength, and so on, powered by anything from rubber bands and clockwork to steam and gasoline. Their brains are just small computers, running a few basic evil programs. To command them, I've recreated great leaders from the past. I've got over fifty Napoleons now, each one as clever as the original, but even better because they don't eat or sleep or give me any backtalk, or get poisoned by the British."

"You know, if you put this much effort into something constructive, you could be a great man."

"Now you sound like my mother. Here, let me show you how I make my troops."

He led me into his factory. It was a huge low building that looked like an airplane factory. Its floor was covered with endless rows of what looked like oversized copying machines.

"Right now these machines are busy making my standard model troops, but they can be programmed to reproduce just about anything. I'll show you how it works."

He walked over to some bins and looked inside.

"First, we make sure the raw material receptacles are at acceptable levels, and… they are."

"Hey," I said, "is this why your robberies in Central City were of warehouses and chemical plants, instead of banks and jewelry stores?"

"Sure. I don't need money. But I'm always running low on raw materials. Can't ever have too much."

He sat down at one of the machines and tapped out a few commands on the keyboard. Then he stood up.

"The software will take over from here. The computer directs the making of the creature. I just have to let it know what I want."

The entire process only took a couple of minutes. After the machine signaled that the operation was complete, a perfect copy of me slid out of the machine and sat up.

"Huh?" I said.

"What?" I replied.

CHAPTER NINE

I was looking at an exact copy of myself. We stared at each other with our mouths hanging open. Then we both smiled. Then we both looked worried. I didn't know what to think. And I didn't know what to think either.

"Say," I said slowly, in stereo, "that looks a little like me."

"It is you. An exact duplicate. The only difference is in the weight. He's mostly foam core, titanium, and elbow macaroni, with a few simple electric motors to make him go." He turned to one of his minions. "Dispose of this."

The assistant chopped the copy of me up with a hatchet, as the copy said things like: "Hey, what are you doin'?" and "Oh, a wise-guy, eh?" and "Careful with that hatchet," then dumped the pieces into a recycling bin. I winced. Even when you know it's not you being chopped up, there's a part of you that's thinking: bullshit, that's me all right.

"I can see how you could make a copy of me,"

I said, "since you've got me here to study. But how did you make a copy of Napoleon?"

"I'll show you that in a moment. First, let me show you my Unholy Army. I think you'll love it."

"I know I will."

He took me out on a veranda, pressed a button, and moments later a grand review began.

For over an hour troops marched smartly by, turning and saluting Overkill as they passed. None of them saluted me, but a few of them nodded. The majority of them were the same type of creature I had encountered in Central City, but there were also toy soldiers, boxing robots, huge battery powered tanks, a platoon of rather cross looking stuffed bears, and thousands of wind-up goblins and orcs.

"You read too much Tolkien," I said.

"You can't read too much Tolkien."

"That's what I meant to say when I spoke."

"I'm glad we agree."

"I'm beginning to think we agree on everything."

"Good."

I watched a few thousand more troops parade by, then said: "It looks to me like you've already got more than enough here to take over the world."

"That's what my accountant keeps saying. But you're both wrong."

"Hey, I might be wrong about something like that, but an accountant, this kind of thing is his business."

"Shut-up. Both of you just shut-up. Besides, you forget the name of my operation. Operation

Overkill. It's important that I have not just enough, not even more than enough, but too much more than enough. Anything less would not be overkill. See the semantics and grammar that are involved?"

"Yeah, of course, but…"

"I've been studying super villains of the past. The biggest mistake all of them made was having just enough of a force to take over the world, but no more. They didn't want to appear gauche, I guess. So what happens? Something goes wrong at substation C, or they lose a handful of men who were supposed to be guarding something important, or one guy doesn't show up for work at the volcano, and their whole operation falls apart. All of a sudden they don't have enough to take over the world. And all because they played it too fine."

"Stupid bastards."

"Super villains historically underestimate the world. A world will fight back. You've got to make allowances for that."

"And you have."

"Yes. That's why Operation Overkill can't fail. My opponents simply have too much to overcome. It doesn't matter how many of my men are grabbed from behind by secret agents and dragged into the bushes. I could have a thousand of my men tied up behind those bushes on the day of the big attack, and I'd still have thousands more than I needed. Overkill is the only way to succeed when it comes to world domination. And Overkill is my name."

"Beautiful."

We walked past a large machine that had a big red handle. "What's that thing?" I asked.

"Doomsday Machine."

"Ah."

"That's in case things don't work out exactly as I've planned. It can destroy the entire universe."

I raised my hand.

"No way to test it, of course," he said, "but I'm confident it will work as it's designed to."

I put down my hand.

"I don't want to seem like a poor sport," he added, "but if I can't rule the universe, I don't want there to be one. Does that make me sound like I'm a poor sport?"

"Not at all. Quite the reverse. Anybody who says you're a poor sport has it backwards."

"I'm relieved to hear you say that. Now, you asked earlier where I got my patterns for Napoleon and Lincoln and so on. Follow me and I'll show you the most amazing part of my operation."

He led me to a large door. Before he opened it he asked: "When we were having dinner, did you notice one of my servants—General Custer, I think it was—come in carrying a tray of hot dogs and suddenly start spinning in a circle against a weird stripy background, finally disappearing with a pop?"

"Yeah. One of those hot dogs was supposed to be for me."

"Do you remember asking me where that bastard went with the hot dogs?"

"Vividly."

He opened the door. "The answer is in here."

We walked in. Overkill stood proudly next to a huge water-nozzle-shaped tunnel.

"What you are looking at is a doorway to the future. Or the past."

"What about the present?"

"No, that's all these other doors. Did you ever see a television show called The Time Nozzle?"

"I think so. Something about two handsome scientists traveling through time with a bad script, wasn't it?"

He nodded. "It was a cheap knockoff of The Time Tunnel. It wasn't very popular and got cancelled after 14 episodes."

"I saw a fantastic episode of Wagon Train once that..."

He interrupted me, impatiently. "After it was cancelled, all of the props from the show were put into storage on the studio lot and forgotten. Then last year they were rediscovered and put up for auction. I had no interest in the smaller props, but I outbid several other super villains for The Time Nozzle itself."

I started telling him about some collectible TV memorabilia I used to have—a Roy Rogers lunchbox and a Lassie paw—but he wasn't interested.

"What viewers in the 1960's didn't realize," he went on, "was that a lot of what they were seeing was real. Studios didn't skimp when it came to production values in those days. Whenever possible they used the real thing, not a mock up. Disney hired the real Zorro, for example, for the show's pilot episode. But it turned out the old fellow had trouble memorizing lines. Couldn't even remember where he lived. They dumped him out in the Valley somewhere and got a younger guy for the series. And I have it on the highest authority—a stuntman told me this—that there was a real Twilight Zone. Rod Serling found it next to his house. He didn't have to write any scripts at all. Just grabbed actors and threw them in, then turned on the cameras. The show wrote itself. Everyone thought those old TV shows were just fantastic entertainment, but they were more than that. They were up to 10% real."

"Wait, are you trying to tell me that The Time Nozzle actually worked?"

"Works," he corrected me. "Present tense. When the show was originally filmed, the actors felt they couldn't get 'into' their parts if the machine didn't actually work." He snorted derisively. "As if it mattered whether they were 'into' their parts or not. Just say the damn lines."

"I hate actors too."

"So handymen at the studio worked on it until they made it operational to a certain extent. It never worked perfectly, but the show's writers incorporated its flaws into their storylines. It was really a remarkable achievement. The epitome of prop technology. Now I've got it, and I've been using it to bring famous people back from the past so I can blueprint them and make copies."

"Why make copies? If you have Napoleon here, why not just keep him here to run your army in person? That's what I would do with my Napoleon."

"I tried that, but The Time Nozzle kept dragging the originals back to their own time, or sending them to the Alamo or the deck of the Titanic or something. Didn't you see the series, Burly?"

"Oh, yeah. That's right."

"Just about every famous person in history ended up on the deck of the Titanic, thanks to this machine. That's why the damn thing sank. Too many famous people on it."

"Now we know the rest of the story."

"Yeah. So, anyway, while I have them here, I make copies. Sometimes they're still around after I no longer need them. That's why you saw Sitting Bull dusting the furniture in the living room and Al Capone out on the lawn shooting weeds. But the machine will reverse itself eventually and they'll pop back to their own time. The sooner that happens the better as far as I'm concerned. The originals get tiresome after awhile. They all think they're big-shots and want to run the island, not clean toilets. I've got the original Lincoln locked in the Purple Room over there. I hated to do it. I've always enjoyed our conversations. That guy is almost as unprincipled as I am. But he won't learn to mind his own business. He keeps trying to free my army. Don't touch that."

"I just wanted to see how it worked. Can we bring back the dinosaurs? Or does it have to be a famous dinosaur?"

Overkill thought about this. "It would be easier if he was famous. But I don't want anybody messing around with the controls right now. I'm close to finalizing a deal with a company in the year 2265 to ship an army of future fighters here. A half million of them. They are the ultimate mechanical men. They have built-in guns, knives, torpedoes, lasers, everything. Like walking Swiss army knives. They're self-maintaining, and can eat anything. So once you start them up, they can fight forever. They'll be the backbone of my army. The elite fighting core. Once they're here, I'll be ready to take over the world."

"What's the hold up?"

"Medical insurance and contributions to pension funds for the fighters that I don't particularly want to pay."

"Damn unions."

"Yeah. But we'll work it out. Well, you've seen it all now. What do you think?"

I didn't hesitate. "I think there's only one thing you need that you don't have."

"What's that?"

"A Flying Detective."

He stared at me, first with astonishment, then with suspicion.

"You want to join my organization? You want to help me take over the world?"

"Yep."

"Why?"

"I'd like to be on the winning side for once. And I don't see how you can lose."

He wasn't sure he believed me at first. He thought it might be a trick. One of the pictures he had of me on the wall—the one of me trying to remember whether I had eaten yet or not—made me look pretty damned tricky. But it wasn't a trick. Nobody was going to stop this guy, as near as I could tell. If he was going to be number one man in the world, I wouldn't mind being number two.

It took a lot to convince him I was on the level. I had to take several different lie detector tests, say "Yes, really" after he had said "Really?" and sign an affidavit in the presence of a notary public, but he finally believed me. I think it was the affidavit that did it. You can't lie on those things. Those things are notarized. Once he was convinced, he pumped my hand enthusiastically.

"This is fine! Outstanding news! Now nothing can stop us! What a team we'll make! The two most formidable men in the world fighting side by side! You can use your regular costume, of course, though I think you should have 'Overkill's Flying Detective' printed on your cape."

"Fine."

"And you should have a better weapon than that .38 you usually carry. Have a look over there in that pile. See if you can find something you like better."

I went over to a pile of strange looking weapons and rummaged around, finally picking out a particularly deadly looking little number, then walked back to Overkill.

"I guess I'll take this one. What is it?"

"That's a machine knife. The Pokemaster 5000. You can stab 1500 guys a minute with that. And because it's a knife and not a gun, you never run out of ammunition. No reloading. You could have single-handedly won World War II with one of those."

"I would have gotten my name in the papers if I'd done that."

He nodded. "In capital letters."

I tripped on the carpet and landed on Overkill, somehow accidentally turning on the Pokemaster as I fell. His lifeless and incredibly poked body collapsed onto an alarm and set it off. I was stunned, but not as stunned as Overkill was, judging by the look on what was left of his face.

As more alarms started going off around the fortress, each one setting off the next, I noticed I was still stabbing Overkill in the chest. This panicked me and I tried to turn the machine off, but only managed to turn it up so it was going faster. Pieces of flesh were flying all over the room. I finally got it turned off. Then I checked his pulse, which had rolled under the couch. He was dead all right. He was more than dead. I had made mincemeat out of him. If I were a clever man, I would say I had "overkilled" him.

I was pretty upset. I'd just wasted a lot of time buttering up this guy. Time I wasn't going to get back. Plus, now I was out of a very plush, probably very high paying, job. I didn't know how much the number two man in the world got paid, but I imagined it was something pretty good. The loss of that big paycheck hurt.

I checked in his pockets and took his wallet, his keys, and a few other odds and ends that caught my fancy. I know readers may look askance at this, but I figured since I'd killed the guy, robbing him wouldn't make it much worse. I'm pretty sure he would have wanted me to rob him after I killed him anyway.

There were alarms going off all over the fortress, and running feet approaching the room, so I figured I'd better get out of there fast before anyone saw what I'd done. Pausing only to steal a few more things from Overkill's body, including a shiny black ring I'd been admiring during dinner, I stood up to go. It was too late. I had stolen one thing too many.

The door opened and a couple of dozen armed guards came in and stood staring at me. Finally one of them spoke.

"Orders, sir?"

"Who, me?"

"Yes. Do you have any orders?"

"Uh… yeah. Wait here."

"Yes, New Master."

I carefully edged past them and ran down the stairs.

CHAPTER TEN

When I got out of the fortress, I had just sense enough to realize I should move as calmly as possible, and try not to arouse any more suspicion than I usually do. So I stopped running and looking over my shoulder and whimpering "oh God oh God oh God," and forced myself to slow down to a frightened saunter, whistling a frightened song.

I made my way past a group of creatures who were working on the lawn. As I passed them, I gave them the thumbs up. They, somewhat confusedly, returned the thumbs up.

There was a small launch at the dock that seemed ready to go, so I stepped aboard. The captain of the craft, who was a dead ringer for Captain Queeg, except for the big key in his back, approached me, frowning.

I tried to act as businesslike as possible. I was here on business. I wasn't escaping. "Overkill told me to take the boat into town for," I said. "He wanted me to get."

The captain didn't seem to mind that my

sentences were incomplete, or that I was sweating like an escaped pig. He just saluted smartly and gave orders to cast off.

On the way to the mainland I kept looking behind us to see if we were being followed. I did this so often, the crewmen started doing it too. But there was no sign of pursuit. Relieved, I took a look around the boat to see if there was anything to eat. I don't know about you, but running for my life after I've killed somebody makes me hungry. I felt like I could kill and eat a horse. I found some strawberries in the pantry and ate them. I don't think anyone ever missed them.

They let me off at the 1st Avenue Pier and asked if they should wait for me. Or maybe follow me. I told them that wasn't necessary, to go back home. I would tell Overkill what a fine job they had done, and recommend them all for important promotions. They saluted again and pushed off back to the island.

I don't think I've ever run so fast as I did for the first half a block. Then I don't think I've ever laid down on the sidewalk for so long. I decided to walk the rest of the way home at a more leisurely pace.

For the next few days I was a little jumpy. I kept expecting someone to come looking for me. But no one did. This surprised me, because usually when you kill somebody, lots of people come looking for you. They want to talk to you about what you did. But that didn't happen this time.

After awhile, I started to relax. Then I started

to get bored. Nothing was going on in the city, crime-wise. Overkill had monopolized crime to such an extent that all of the city's original or "classic" criminals had either moved away or retired. Now, with Overkill out of the picture too, there wasn't much for a detective to do.

I put small ads in the paper that said I was "At Liberty," but nothing happened. Except someone finally put a small ad next to mine that said: "Good."

I was hired briefly to take pictures of a guy's wife in a compromising situation with another man. I got the pictures, but it turned out the guy who hired me wasn't her husband, after all. He was just some guy who collected pictures like that. The police were pretty understanding about the whole thing and I only spent a month in jail.

Finally, just to ease the boredom and get a little cash coming in, I looked up that guy I met at the Super Villain Club who kept saying he wasn't the Devil. He wasn't at the club, but I finally tracked him down. He had a house in a lake of fire, though he said that didn't prove anything. I told him I wouldn't mind doing a little part-time work for him on a free-lance basis, nothing permanent, if he had anything he wanted me to do.

So that's how I found myself prowling the streets in my car late at night looking for souls and trying to talk people into being bad. It wasn't very difficult work. I'd see people buying something in a store, for example, and point out they could save a lot of money if they stole that object instead of buying it. It would represent a 100% savings. A lot of people had never thought of that. After talking to me, they put their money back in their pockets, along with a lot of other stuff. Or I'd make some old guy a successful baseball player overnight, and he'd ask how he could ever repay me, and I'd say funny you should mention that, and start hauling out the burning contracts.

I felt good that I was helping people out and getting business for my employer, and making a little money for myself besides. But overall life was pretty dull for me now, especially dull when I compared it to the kind of lifestyle Overkill had had. That guy really had it made.

Thinking about Overkill's great life reminded me that I'd stolen his wallet. There hadn't been much money in it. Just a few bucks. Hardly worth desecrating his body for, really. When am I going to learn? But I hadn't bothered to look through the rest of the wallet—all the little compartments and secret flaps. Maybe there were some credit cards or IDs I could use. I could pretend I was him at a store. Get some stuff for free. I started to look through the wallet with this in mind, when a thought struck me. I looked at my hand. On it was the shiny black ring I'd stolen from Overkill's hand.

I suddenly realized how I'd gotten off the island without being challenged. And why all the creatures had called me Master. And why two of them had approached me seeking raises in salary. Overkill's ring was bigger and shinier than the similar rings his creatures were wearing. This must be the Ring of Power. The One Ring That Rules Them All. I told Overkill he read too much Tolkien, but he wouldn't listen to me.

If it was a Ring of Power, that meant that as long as I wore it all of Overkill's creatures would treat me as if I was him. So I could, if I dared try it, take Overkill's place on the island, and live in luxury like he had been doing, happily ever after, like he did. The more I thought about it, the more I began to think I could pull it off. I knew it was wrong, but I also knew it would work. I knew two things about it.

I was still hesitating—it was a risky move. There's a downside to doing anything that's really wrong—but then I got the afternoon mail. It contained a gas bill, a jury summons, fourteen assorted other bills, and a letter from someone I'd never met in my life saying I was an asshole. I guess he found my name on a list of assholes or something. That decided it. I tossed the mail in the trash, put on my hat, adjusted my Ring of Power, and headed back to the island.

When I stepped off the boat, I held the Ring of Power up high so everybody could see it, and walked cautiously across the lawn towards the fortress, ready to turn and run for it at the first sign of opposition. A number of eyes turned my way, and some teeth, but no one tried to stop me.

The guards I had told to wait in Overkill's laboratory were still there. Most of them were asleep on their feet, but a couple were reading or exchanging anecdotes of the "you think this is a long time to be standing here doing nothing? You should have been around for Oktoberfest last year" variety. The moment I entered they snapped to attention.

I hesitated. This was the moment. "Are you still waiting for orders from me?" I asked.

"Yes, New Worried Master."

"Good. Uh... resume your normal duties."

They acknowledged my order with something a little too close to a Nazi salute, for my money. I didn't know if they were being wise-guys or not, but I made a mental note to change that salute to something a little less controversial. For the time being I just returned the salute and said "sieg heil."

I found Overkill's desk and looked through his papers, to see if I could get a better idea of how this place worked, and what exactly his plans had been. He had told me some of it, but I needed to know more if I was going to take his place. I picked up a few stray bits of information, here and there. Overkill's first name was Orville, for example. But most of what I found I couldn't understand. There were sheets full of numbers, which can mean anything, of course, and maps with countries circled and the word "Destroy" or "Use Plan 9" stamped on them, and sheaves of legal papers that seemed to be trying to justify what he was doing by claiming it fell under Section 3 of The Homestead Act. Finally I gave up. I just didn't get what it was all about. Oh, well. I've never really known how the detective business works either, and that hasn't stopped me. Just made me bad at it.

I spent the rest of the afternoon looking around my new home. It was an improvement over my one bedroom house in Central City, I'll say that for it. This place had everything. All the comforts of home: moats, parapets, you name it. And everything was huge.

The master bedroom had a massive bed in it that Overkill said used to belong to the 7th Cavalry. It had about a dozen beautiful mechanical dames reclining on it, oiling each other. They asked if there was anything I wanted, and I said there certainly was, and outlined my wants in detail for them. They slapped my face, like all women do. But they looked scared after they had done it. That was an improvement anyway. I decided I was going to like being a super villain.

Everywhere I went in the fortress I was confronted by anxious creatures who asked me what they should do now. They needed more orders. I just told them to keep doing what they were doing, and don't bother the boss. They obeyed instantly, which is what us bosses like. So I guess that's how I ended up with all those weather machines and bowling alleys. I had thousands of them.

When all the detectives in the dungeon found out I was running things now, they demanded to be let out. I started to let them out, with them saying come on, hurry up stupid, pointing out that they didn't have all day, when I suddenly decided maybe they had better stay in there for awhile. I wasn't completely sure which side of the law I was on now. And I was starting to see Overkill's point of view. Maybe the world would be better off if it was controlled by one evil man, instead of many. It was a thought worth thinking about, anyway. In the meantime the detectives would be safe in the dungeon, I told them. No one could get them there. They said that wasn't the point. They weren't worried about someone getting them. They were... but I didn't hear any more, because I had already slammed the dungeon door.

They made several attempts to escape from my clutches after that, using the only materials available to them, but I stopped that by spraying ant poison around the outside of the dungeon. That ant robot of theirs was stupid anyway.

I don't believe I've ever had a better time than I had over the next couple of weeks.

I roamed the island wearing a Hawaiian shirt and Magellan's helmet, smoking a big cigar, with a can of imported beer in one hand and an unresponsive mechanical babe on the other.

There were plenty of things to do to keep yourself occupied. You could swim in the pool, make the invisible shield go up and down, play tennis with Joan of Arc, make an example of somebody, anything. And I did them all.

All good things must come to an end, they say, because that's the way this crappy world of ours works. But I didn't expect my good thing to end so soon. All of a sudden things started to go wrong all over the island: dungeon leaks, laser cannons going dead and needing to be recharged, parapet trouble, and so on. The usual homeowner problems, but on a much grander scale. I found I was spending all day, every day, making repairs and trying to get parapet repairmen and moat cleaners from the mainland to show up when they said they were going to.

Then one day I had to shut down the island's cloaking device because it had started malfunctioning and I couldn't find my way to the bathroom or see myself in the mirror anymore. I didn't worry too much about it being off, because there was no real need for it right now anyway. It's not like I was hiding from anybody. It's not like there was anybody after me. It's not like that.

That night I was having dinner with some of my mechanical babes and the real Woodrow Wilson. Overkill had brought him forward in time to make slipshod treaties with his enemies that would look good on paper and then turn out to be crap, and he hadn't popped back to his own time period yet.

He was telling me how he did too keep us out of war, he kept us out of war for months, and I was telling him to shut-up and eat, when suddenly there was an earsplitting crash and glass shattered onto the table from the skylight. The glass was followed by a drunken man in a shabby tuxedo. The man groaned for a moment, then struggled into a crouching position in the chili and leveled a Luger at me.

"Hands up, Overkill," said the world famous British Secret Service Agent Fred Foster.

CHAPTER ELEVEN

I had heard of Fred Foster, of course. Everyone had. He was Britain's most famous and successful "double-oh" spy. So famous he wasn't a very good spy anymore. It's almost impossible to sneak up on an enemy when you're surrounded by screaming fans and writers waving spec scripts. Try it.

And he wasn't much use as a spy anymore anyway, even without the fame. The fabulous Cold War lifestyle he had led all those years had finally caught up with him. His liver was shot—one drink and he would completely lose control of his motor functions—and he couldn't lay in wait successfully anymore because of his smoker's cough, ("I think the coughing is coming from behind this bush, Alexei"). And his eyesight was starting to fail him, but he was too vain to wear the giant clown glasses his eyes required.

Foreign agents were well aware of all these faults, of course. They no longer feared Foster. To them, he was just a joke. Eventually even the British Secret Service became aware of his physical problems, when they captured some enemy jokebooks.

He was sent to rehab several times, but it never did any good. He just came back drunker and a bigger and funnier joke than before. And every time he was sent out on an assignment, the British Empire got smaller.

Finally his license to kill was suspended, and he stopped getting the plum assignments. To his mortification, he watched younger agents with better functioning livers and bladders getting all the glamorous assignments, while he was reduced to opening the door of MI5 for them as they bowled off on their next action-filled adventure.

I found out later that he had begged as a personal favor from his old friend Z, who ran the Secret Service now that the rest of the alphabet was dead, to give him one last chance and let him handle the Overkill matter. That favor had been reluctantly granted, and now here he was standing in my chili.

"I'm not Overkill," I said.

"Maybe not, but my supervisor won't know the difference. Hands in the air."

I was aware of his current reputation. I held my arms straight out from my sides like I was welcoming my wandering boy home. "You mean like this?"

"No," he said, raising his hands high in the air, "like this."

He overbalanced badly and fell backwards onto the table where he instantly fell asleep in the forks. I snapped my fingers and my guards picked him up and carried him away.

I didn't have him thrown in the dungeon. I'd seen enough Fred Foster Secret Agent movies to know that a super villain, which is what I was now, I guess, was supposed to treat enemy agents like honored guests. Give them a fancy room, let them hobnob with your beautiful women, and get a good long look at all your defenses and secret plans. I didn't know why this was so—it made more sense to just kill them, or at least lock them up—but this was the way it was supposed to be done, so I did it that way. For awhile, anyway.

As a house guest, Foster left a lot to be desired. I'd have him for dinner to exchange witticisms and clever barbs, for example, and he'd either pass out mid-barb, or suddenly leap at me, knocking me and my babes over, and then start pounding on us with his fists.

He kept trying to get me to tell him my plan so he could foil it and get his reputation back. I kept telling him I didn't have a plan, and didn't care about his stupid reputation anyway, but that just seemed to make him surly. He'd drink some more and tell me I was insane, but I usually couldn't understand most of what he was saying because his mouth was so far down in his drink. I'd mostly just hear a bunch of bubbles.

His presence in the fortress got more annoying every day. He kept opening, and answering, all my mail before I could get to it, stealing diagrams of my defenses that I needed to show to repairmen, and keeping me awake half the night, every night, telling me I was nuts. He was the one who was nuts, if you ask me.

I could have killed him, I suppose, but he seemed so pathetic it didn't seem sporting. Plus, he might be an insurance policy I could cash in later. And, I almost forgot, killing is wrong.

But after he had jauntily tossed himself onto my hat rack for the twentieth time, and I had to once again stop what I was doing to get him down, I decided I'd had enough of the guy. I locked him up in the dungeon with the detectives. It wasn't the way you were supposed to treat secret agents, I knew I would probably get letters about it, but at that point I just didn't care.

Even locked in a dungeon he found ways to cause me trouble. He insulted one of my guards so much the guard quit and went to work for some other maniac. And after I had finally gotten the detectives calmed down into a nice sullen silence by putting a television in there, Foster got them all riled up again by changing the channels too much. After a couple of near riots, which caused $150 worth of damage to my dungeon door, I finally had them all chained up. And I put double chains on Foster.

Well I don't know how you can fall out of a dungeon, but I guess if you're drunk enough you can do it. Foster did it. Suddenly he was just out, staggering across the island, and into the water. He struggled his way out of the water and flew in a hang-glider across the island and into the water on the other side. Then he went by again, this time on the hood of a runaway Aston Martin.

Finally he began bouncing grimly towards the fortress on a pogo stick. I don't know where these secret agents get all their gadgets from at a moment's notice. If I wanted to fly around in a hang-glider or bounce on a pogo stick at somebody, I'd have to go downtown and buy those things, then wait for them to be delivered to my home. Secret agents just suddenly have them. How do you beat somebody like that?

Before my guards could get to Foster he had bounced into the island's power station. A few moments later he re-emerged and started speaking into a microphone he had apparently secreted away in a false back to his head. I didn't like this. I didn't know who he was talking to, but he seemed a little too sober all of a sudden.

My alert guards rushed up and grabbed him, tearing off the back of his head and dashing it to the ground. I signaled them to bring him to me.

"Too bad, Overkill," he smirked as he was thrown down in front of me. I was surprised to note that, for the first time since I had met him, he wasn't slurring his words. He had obviously dried out partially in the dungeon. "Your operation is finished."

"I'm still not Overkill," I reminded him. "And what do you mean my operation is finished?"

As if in answer, the lights suddenly went out all over the island.

"I've killed your island, Overkill. It's dead. Your power plant, your cloaking device, and your laser cannons. They're all out of commission. And I've jammed your invisible shield so it can't be closed.

There'll be a government fleet here in a few minutes, and they'll be able to walk right in with nothing to stop them. When they do, I'll be handing you over to them personally."

He pulled a cigarette lighter out of his pocket and snapped it open. It quickly transformed into a miniature machine gun. He had it pointed at himself instead of me, but it was still a dangerous situation. Guns can be turned around. I had to think fast.

"Have a drink?" I asked.

CHAPTER TWELVE

Once he had accepted the first martini, it didn't take long to get Foster successfully re-inebriated and safely locked back up in the dungeon. I put a half dozen chains on him this time, as well as a granite slab and a small guard. Then I took a moment to consider my situation. It didn't look good.

If I had really been Overkill, I probably wouldn't have been worried about a government attack. I'm sure a real super villain would have known exactly what to do—who to kill, what cities to target for annihilation, what threats to yell over a bullhorn, and so on. I didn't know any of that stuff. So I figured I'd better pack.

Before I could get the first Rembrandt smooshed down into a suitcase, the fortress began to shake and plaster started falling from the ceiling. I ran to the nearest window and looked out. The island was being pounded from all sides by federal gunboats and police cruisers. They were really socking it to me. Even worse, almost every shot was blowing up something I had just gotten repaired at great expense. It would take weeks to get repairmen out here to fix them again. I found myself muttering kill maim frighten destroy under my breath.

I used a signaling device to contact the fleet and let them know that there was no need for all the fireworks. I told them I wasn't Overkill, and anyway I was quitting. They responded that I certainly was quitting. "Quitting to prison." I signaled back that they should get some new writers.

The shelling increased. I kept signaling frantically and with growing incoherence, suggesting a truce, a peace conference, an armistice, every euphemism for surrender I could think of. I even, in my desperation, advanced the idea that maybe if the U.S. government's theme song were combined with mine into one beautiful song, then maybe we could be friends. Or maybe if I married the government's daughter, it would unite the two warring sides forever more. They ignored these signals, and by this point I wasn't paying much attention to them either. When I noticed that I was signaling that the attacking ships should go screw themselves, I stopped signaling entirely. Those kinds of signals don't solve anything. They just make things worse.

Since they didn't want to talk, and there was nowhere for me to run, it looked like I was going to have to fight. Fortunately, I had thousands of Unholy Army men at my disposal.

After a brief strategy conference with Napoleon #47 and U.S. Grant #6, I ordered my fighting forces out into battle, for the glory of good old Unhappy Island, or whatever the hell it was called.

This is when I found out that I was supposed to be regularly maintaining my troops. The ones that ran on batteries shuffled out of the fortress to do battle, rather than charge. And many of them just stood there and made clicking sounds. Some of the steam powered ones had clogged pipes and blew up when they were switched on. A great many of the wind-up ones had misplaced their keys, and lied to me about it, saying they had never been issued keys. And I lost track of how many vital rubber bands had snapped through neglect.

I could see why Overkill had wanted to get those advanced fighters from the future. They were self-maintaining, and... you might think me dense, but it wasn't until I was thinking about this that I remembered The Time Nozzle, and the future fighters waiting to be transported to the island.

I raced into the laboratory where The Time Nozzle was located and turned it on. Overkill had told me that the machine was already set to receive a half million fully armed fighters as soon as he agreed to the health and pension benefits the fighters were demanding, so I looked around for an "I agree" button on the console. This was no time for economy. I'd screw them out of their pensions later. I couldn't find a button that said "I agree," so I just started hitting every button in sight that had an agreeable look to it.

Nothing happened. Fortunately, I know how

to handle balky machines. First you say "Aw, come on!" then you bang on the controls, then you throw small objects at the machine, then you give it a good swift kick in the slats. Then the machine is repaired.

I had to hurry though. The government troops had landed and were making rapid progress across my lawn. So I banged on the controls furiously, then started throwing things into The Time Nozzle to see if that would get things moving. I threw coffee mugs, staplers, ashtrays, and some books from Overkill's collection of first editions: "A Clockwork Orange," Orwell's "1984," and "The Life of Lincoln." They were all pretty valuable, I guess, but I didn't have time to count the cost. I needed to get that machine going. Unfortunately, nothing happened.

I heard the sounds of battle move inside the fortress itself, past my scandalized butler, and up the stairs. Now I really didn't have much time.

I kicked at the entrance to The Time Nozzle, but that didn't do anything. So I raced into its spirally interior. There didn't seem to be any machinery I could kick in there, but those stripes looked like they might be the problem, so I started fiercely kicking them.

Suddenly the door to the laboratory burst open and Fred Foster came roaring in. He spotted me in the middle of The Time Nozzle and charged in after me.

As we were wrestling around on the floor of the machine, one of us must have accidentally kicked the right stripe, because all of a sudden thousands of eight foot tall fully armored fighters from the future began streaming through the tunnel past us—the rockets on their shoulders gleaming, their ten inch metal fangs bared, and their fierce faces wearing the contented looks of death machines who knew they had medical insurance they could count on. I guess one of those buttons I had hit on the console must have been the "I accept" button I was looking for after all. I was delighted. My elite troops were here! Now I could fight back against the world that had been causing me so much trouble! Kill Maim Frighten Destroy!

As the last of the troops hurtled by, Foster and I began to be pulled slowly in the other direction, farther into The Time Nozzle. I tried to get up and get out of there, but Foster continued to grapple with me drunkenly and wouldn't let go, reminding me all the time that I was insane, that my plan would never work, and that I was mad.

Our speed through the tunnel increased and then suddenly we were pinwheeling around against a weird colored background, still fighting. Finally we disappeared with a couple of angry pops.

CHAPTER THIRTEEN

I shot out of the end of what seemed like a big sewer pipe. A moment later Foster shot out of the same pipe and began drunkenly grappling with me.

"You're mad, Overkill," he said, as he slugged away clumsily at me, somehow, in his struggles, managing to step on his own face, and kick two of his own teeth out.

I threw him off of me and kicked him in the back of the head for luck just as a police officer hurried up.

"Here! What's going on?" He demanded. "Stop that, you two!"

I looked the policeman over. There was something odd about him. I didn't know what it was at first, then I realized it was that Lincoln beard of his. Hardly regulation, I thought. Oh well. I'm not running the department.

I pointed at Foster. "There he is, officer."

"Who?"

"The guy who's been causing all the trouble around here."

The policemen picked up Foster by the collar. "Are you the one?"

Foster stopped singing and eyed the policeman, then told him his plan would never work.

"Right," said the policeman grimly. He began roughly dragging Foster off, telling him he was taking him to jail, and no, they wouldn't be stopping at a liquor store on the way, and it didn't matter who was buying.

With Foster out of the way, I took a moment to assess my situation. I didn't know where I was, as usual, but wherever I was it had to be better than the place I'd just left. It just had to be. I made sure nobody could follow me by kicking the end of The Time Nozzle to pieces. I knew I'd never regret doing that. Kicking things to pieces is the kind of thing you never regret. (But see Chapter Sixteen!)

I started walking towards what looked like the center of town. Judging from the streamlined office buildings and the tramps with fins on them, I figured I must be at some point in the future. The past didn't have any streamlined buildings that I could recall. And the buildings I remembered as being new in the early 21st century were now quite dilapidated, and full of finned tramps.

Another tip-off that I had passed into the future was the strange kind of outfits everybody was wearing. They looked like something out of "A Clockwork Orange," except with Lincoln style hats and beards. I also saw a flashing time and temperature sign that said it was May 23, 2265, and a huge banner that said "Welcome To The Future," though on closer inspection I found out the banner was just part of an ad campaign for salted nuts.

I'd been to the future before, of course. I've been all over the space/time continuum at one time or another, though never, as near as I can recall, on purpose. But I'd never been to this particular era.

The whole place was Lincoln crazy, that was the first thing you noticed about it. Practically everybody was wearing Lincoln hats and Lincoln style beards. There were statues of Lincoln everywhere. Sometimes the statues seemed to be looking at you, even calling up people about you. It was all a bit much, if you ask me. I mean, I kind of like Lincoln myself, but come on!

The other obvious difference from my time was that everything was so small now. It was miniaturization gone wild. In an average citizen's pocket you could find virtually everything he would ever need, including his house and his grave. And of course, all of these essentials were very inexpensive, since they were so completely worthless.

The only place you could find anything big was in the museums, where there were all kinds of displays of "ancient" 21st century handicrafts, like comically big hats that covered your whole head. And microscopes you could see without a microscope.

How this all came about is anybody's guess.

It was hard to get any solid facts about this time period or what led up to it, because of the miniaturization craze. All books, newspapers, magazines, and so on, had all been long ago converted to digits and placed in digital information storage systems, which over the years had gotten smaller and smaller until finally they were gone. So nobody knew much of anything anymore. They knew what they liked, but that was about it. And they liked Lincoln.

Since I was in the future, I expected to find some of the things George Orwell had predicted in his prophetic novel "1984." I didn't like to think that Orwell had just been shitting us. But I needn't have worried. A few of his prophesies were right on the button. There were Thought Police roaming the streets, most of them dressed like William H. Seward, for some reason. But it was relatively easy to deal with them. They would say something like: "You there! What are you thinking?" And all you had to say was: "I'm thinking about how great the government is," and they would say: "Very well. Carry on."

The language had been tampered with too, as Orwell predicted. You couldn't say "tax refund" anymore, for example. No such word. I didn't mind. The fewer words there are, the smarter I sound. If we ever get down to just one word, I'm sure I'll be able to say it as well as anybody.

As I walked around, I was surprised by the obvious lack of a population problem. I was always told back in the ignorant past, where I came from, that eventually there would be too many people.

This plainly hadn't happened. If anything, there were fewer people in the streets than there were in my time. I wondered why. An old guy who couldn't move fast enough anymore to get away from me said it was because of the Equality Movement. Mankind had always been striving to make everyone equal. Once the government had finally succeeded in making us all equal in every way, it started wondering if it needed so many of us. That's when the liquidations started.

I was also curious, and growing increasingly so, to know where a guy could get something to eat around here. I tried buying something at a restaurant, but they only took "Credits," whatever those were. I held out some dollar bills, but they said those weren't credits. I held up a button. That wasn't a credit. I shook my fist at them. No credits there either. Eventually I found out a "credit" was a screwdriver. I checked my pockets, but I didn't have any "credits" on me. I went to a hardware store and they had a screwdriver all right, but they wanted a shitload of screwdrivers for it. Kind of a Catch-22 there.

Fortunately, I knew where I could find some food. I spent the rest of the day digging up time capsules all over town and eating anything that was still edible inside. The chocolate bars and cookies were still good, though the TV dinners had thawed and gone bad long ago. There were other examples of 21st Century culture in the time capsules, of course, but I tossed all that stuff aside. It was the food I was after.

I knew where all the time capsules were,

because I had helped bury them. After my first trip through time, I had talked the city fathers into burying dozens of them all over town. Time Capsule Week in Central City was my idea. I didn't care about preserving our stupid culture for halfwit future generations or anything stupid or halfwit like that. I just wanted to make sure that the next time I traveled through time I would have some food stashed somewhere.

I didn't have anyplace to stay, so I made myself comfortable under an overpass and whiled away the time drinking time capsule wine and singing songs of my fathers.

After I'd been there awhile, I noticed I wasn't alone. I was surrounded by a half a dozen young punks who were dressed at the height of teen fashion. They were laughing and smecking and govreeting at me. I looked up at them.

A half hour later we were driving along in our Durango 95, playing hogs of the road. Those kids of the future sure know how to have a good time, I'll say that for them.

It was during one of our Surprise Visits—this one to the home of a writer of subversive literature (the bastard)—that I was hit on the head with a milk bottle by one of my droogs and woke up in a cell at the police station.

I was holding my head and cursing the deceitfulness of future youth, when I noticed I was not alone in the cell. Fred Foster was in there with me.

We were still fighting the next morning when an important looking individual entered our cell.

We let go of each others' entrails and looked him over.

"The President wants to see you, Mr. Burly," he said. "You and your little playmate."

"Are you the President?"

"No."

I digested this information. "Then it sounds like we've got some work to do."

"Yes."

An hour later we were in Washington. The Lincoln motif was even more prevalent there, I noticed. There must have been at least a hundred Lincoln Memorials scattered around town, and all the streets had been renamed Lincoln Avenue.

"Hey, what's with all the Lincoln stuff?" I asked the man who was escorting us.

He didn't answer. I guess he was thinking about something else. Lincoln, probably.

We were escorted into the White House and led up to a large door, which slowly swung open for us.

We walked cautiously through a huge hall towards a flickering light that was visible at one end. When we got closer to the light, we saw that it was a huge ball of fire shooting forty feet up into the air, with Abraham Lincoln's furious face in the flames.

"Four score!" It thundered. "Four score!"

Foster seemed unnerved by the sight. He tried to hide behind himself, somehow ending up with his head stuck in his back pocket.

I wasn't frightened. I had seen the Wizard of Oz a thousand times. I walked across the room to a small curtained area that was off to one side and pulled the curtains open to reveal a much smaller Lincoln. But when it spoke, it wasn't in Lincoln's voice.

"Pretty neat setup, eh, Burly?" asked Overkill.

CHAPTER FOURTEEN

I was surprised to hear Overkill's voice for a number of reasons. For one thing, the last time I had seen him he was dead. And that was 200 years ago. And he had looked a little like Edward G. Robinson then, not a lot like Abe Lincoln.

"Welcome to the 23rd Century, Frank," he said. "It's been a long time. The last time we met, let's see when was it? Oh, yes, I remember now, it's when YOU KILLED ME."

"I've been meaning to apologize about that."

"That was the last time I met anybody, because I was DEAD."

"I'll never forgive myself."

"Nor will I."

"I wish I were never born."

"We all wish that."

My apologies weren't going over very well. I decided to give up on them. "Go on with what you were saying," I said, with a small wave of my hand.

"But I didn't stay dead," he continued. "A strange thing happened. I would call it a miracle, but I don't think God gets involved in stuff like this. It's not His area. I was suddenly conscious again, lying on an operating table, with doctors working on me and comparing my face to a picture of Abraham Lincoln they had on a five dollar bill, and scratching their heads.

"I didn't know what was going on at first. I was a bit disoriented. I mean, one minute you're in Heaven, the next…"

"Wait. You were in Heaven?"

"Yes." He saw my look. "I sent someone a Christmas card once."

"That's all it takes?"

"Yes. Now will you let me finish my story?"

"Oh, okay. Sorry."

"I didn't know why they were going to so much trouble to bring me back to life. But I gradually pieced it all together. It seems the world had lost its way in the 23rd Century, or thought it had, and decided it needed a complete makeover. Somehow the copy of 'The Life of Lincoln' from my library had turned up here, as well as my copies of 'A Clockwork Orange' and '1984.'" He looked at me. I didn't say anything.

"All other books had been lost for years, thanks to miniaturization, and my three books were avidly read by everybody. Gradually it began to dawn on them that the future they had created wasn't nearly as interesting as the future that had been prophesized. All anybody was doing around here was just sitting around watching TV and bitching about things. The future was supposed to be more interesting than that. They felt like they had really dropped the ball.

"They began patterning their present on the prophesies of the future they found in 'A Clockwork Orange' and '1984.' And the Lincoln book told them who they should get to run the place right. They used a time scanning device to locate Lincoln in the past. The last place his body showed up was on my island. After you killed me, by the way, where did you stash my body?"

"In that room you had Lincoln in. It was empty, so I figured it would be a good place to put you. Under the bed. With some old clothes piled on top of you."

He gave me a look.

"Your body didn't fit in with my plans," I said.

He grunted, then continued: "I guess that explains why they thought they were getting Lincoln when they pulled me forward in time. They were a little confused when I didn't look like the pictures of Lincoln they had. In fact, my face didn't look like anything. It was mashed to a pulp." He looked at me again.

"I got upset when I realized I had killed you," I explained.

He grimaced. "But they knew I had to be Lincoln. Their scanning devices did not make mistakes, the manufacturer insisted, or your money back. So, using old photographs and hearsay, they rebuilt me to look as much like Lincoln as they could. Then they turned the world over to me. Gave me absolute power. Told me to fix the place up right. And I have fixed it up right.

It's a perfect world now. For me, anyway. And everyone is happy. Or they'd better be. South Carolina seceded, but I expected that."

I stared at him, impressed. He was actually ruling the world, just like he'd always said he would. And I had thought he was crazy. I could tell him that now. Though I guess I shouldn't have, judging by the look on his face, and the distance he spit out his coffee.

I decided this might be a good time for me to be toddling along. I didn't like the way his head was elongating. "I am glad everything turned out all right for you," I said, shaking his unresponsive hand. "And now, I'll be saying goodbye."

"Stay awhile."

"All right."

He looked up at the boiling ball of flaming gas that now showed he and I chatting amiably. Foster was furiously fighting with it, but getting nowhere.

"Who's your friend?"

"That's Fred Foster, the secret agent. But he's not really my friend. He's just been following me around through time and space trying to kill me."

"Foster, eh? I've heard of him. He can be dangerous when he's sober."

He snapped his fingers and several guards ran up.

"Put Mr. Foster in the Blue Dungeon. I'll deal with him later. Make sure he has plenty to drink."

The guards saluted, quickly apprehended Foster and dragged him, singing, out of the room.

Overkill turned back to me. "Now let's go to my Revenge Room."

"Lead on."

"I built it just for you."

"Sounds great."

He led me out to the elevators. As we walked, he glanced at me approvingly. "I see you quit smoking, as I advised."

"Yes, but only because nobody seems to make cigarettes anymore. The only cigarettes left are in museums, and I've smoked all of those."

We took the elevator down as far as it would go, then he graciously escorted me into the bowels of the building.

I felt I should keep complimenting this dangerous man. "Nice bowels in this building."

"Thank you."

He led me through some dim corridors to a particularly nasty looking door that was covered with warning signs. I didn't bother to read what they said, but it was something about not going inside.

We went inside.

"I've got everything I want now," he said quietly, as the door closed. "Including the revenge I've always sought on the man who killed me. Come, let me show you my DeathBox."

"All right."

As he began leading me towards what sounded like my doom, I had a sudden inspiration. I realized I was still wearing Overkill's shiny black ring. The One Ring That Rules Them All. I held it up so Overkill's guards could see it. Then I pointed at Overkill.

"Seize him!" I commanded.

The guards stared at me stonily. Only one of them made a move to seize Overkill, and he stopped and coughed when he saw he was the only one.

I held the ring higher and moved it a little closer to them. "Seize him, my pretties!"

Still nothing, except that one guy again.

I looked at Overkill. He held up his hand. He was wearing an even bigger ring than I was.

"When I noticed my ring was missing, I figured I'd better make another one," he explained.

Ignoring my offers to trade rings—I wasn't proposing a straight swap. I was willing to throw in some cash—he led me towards a box in the center of the room that was about twice the size of a phone booth.

On the way, we passed something familiar. It was a large machine, with a big red handle.

"I see you've still got your Doomsday Machine," I said.

"Oh, you've got to have a Doomsday Machine. I'd feel naked without one. I mean, what if something went wrong with one of my plans? Stop pulling on the handle, you idiot!"

"I just wanted to see how much play was in it."

"Well, next time just ask me."

"All right. Hey, when are we going to get to the DeathBox?"

"Oh, yeah, I almost forgot."

He guided me over to the box and opened the door. I walked inside and looked around.

"Doesn't look like much," I sniffed.

"Oh, it does the job, I assure you. It bursts each cell in the human body individually, in rapid succession. You'll go off like an atom bomb. And then you will cease to trouble me, in any time period."

"Won't an explosion like that do damage to the building? Or at least to the box?"

"No. The DeathBox is made of the strongest substance known to man: painted iron. It can stand up to anything, even a human body going nuclear. Oh, our ears will ring for awhile around here, but the only thing that will be destroyed is you."

"Oh, okay. I thought I'd spotted a flaw in your plan."

"Well you didn't."

"Fine." I looked around some more. "Hey! There isn't a ventilation shaft in this box."

"No."

"Well, how am I going to get out?"

"You're not."

I looked at him with horror. This was horrible. He started to close the door. I tried to get him to change his mind.

"Wait! You think of yourself as a modern day Abraham Lincoln. Would Lincoln do this? Would Lincoln kill people just to have things his own way? Think man!"

My pleadings fell on deaf ears. Then I tried appealing to his comedy sense.

"How about the old switcheroo?"

"What's that?"

"That's where you say you're going to kill me,

you're going to kill me, you're going to kill me, then you don't kill me. It's hilarious."

"I don't get it."

"Yes you do, look…"

He started closing the door, but he couldn't quite get it closed because my foot was in it. He looked around for a hatchet to chop my foot off. I used the brief respite to make one last appeal.

"You can't do this to me. You're my best friend."

He stared at me. "I'm your best friend?"

"Well… yeah. I only have a few friends. And they all treat me worse than you do. So, yeah, you're my best friend in the whole world."

"That's pathetic."

"Only a true friend would tell me that. Thank you, pal. Now let me out."

He swung the hatchet at my foot and I got it out of the way just in time. Then he slammed the door and bolted it. He looked at me through the door's small window. I made as friendly a face as I could and then pointed it at him. He didn't respond. I kept making my face friendlier and friendlier to the point where both of us were getting kind of nauseated. It was a question of who would puke first. Finally he opened the door.

"I can't do it. Come on out."

I stepped out of the DeathBox, relieved. That was a close one. I had been about to stop looking friendly and start calling him an ugly bastard. But friendship had triumphed just in the nick of time.

I started to thank Overkill for his

magnanimous gesture and assure him he would never regret it. Just then, Fred Foster, Secret Agent, burst into the room, having somehow fallen out of the White House dungeon, and came charging across the room at me.

I tried to duck out of the way, but he crashed into me and I toppled heavily over onto Overkill, driving the hatchet he was holding deep into his chest.

I stood up, shakily, and looked at Overkill. He appeared to be dead. I had killed him again. I looked at Foster, who was lying face down on the floor, singing loudly into the planks.

I tried to give Overkill CPR, but I've never been very good at that, and by the time I was finished, his chest was a mess and his head was gone. It probably rolled somewhere, but I couldn't find it.

I stood up and leaned against the Doomsday Machine lever to think about what I had accidentally done, and figure out what was the smartest thing to do now.

The lever came down with a sharp clunk and the universe started to end.

Everything started to shake and there was a high-pitched "Sqeeeee!" coming from the atoms around me. I didn't like that. That didn't sound right to me. I couldn't get the lever to go back up, and the "sqeeeees" were growing louder and more high-pitched, so I figured I'd better get out of there. I started to run, carefully avoiding the building's security devices which I had apparently also triggered. Lincoln hats were shooting out of walls and big beards and warts were dropping from the ceiling. And all the time I was trying to outrun the end of the universe. What a day!

The door to the outside was locked, apparently shut down by the security system. I ran back the way I had come, looking for another door, or maybe a window. Suddenly I tripped over Overkill's body and went ass over teakettle into the DeathBox. The door slammed shut and the machinery started up, beginning the "Death Process."™

I banged on the door, but it wouldn't open.

I tried taking the machine apart from the inside with a small screwdriver somebody had given me in change, but there had to be at least a million screws in that thing.

I finally gave up and threw the screwdriver against the door. The only other thing I had to throw against the door, unless I wanted to try throwing the screwdriver again, was me, so I threw that. That didn't work either. Nothing was working around here.

The cells in my body were starting to explode, just like Overkill had said they would. At least the DeathBox worked. My nose cells were going first. They were closest to the front of the box, the business end, I guess you'd call it. I probed my nose gingerly with an exploding fingertip. Part of the nose was gone, all right. The best part, too. The part with the holes in it. I clenched my exploding teeth and waited for the end.

Suddenly the machine stopped. I looked out the window and saw that the DeathBox controls had been vaporized along with the rest of the building. The end of the universe had saved me, though probably only temporarily.

Since I only had a small window to look out of, I can't give you a good description of what the end of the universe looked like. But I can imagine what it was like: a horrible shaking everywhere, people running around screaming their heads off, things falling off shelves, workmen dropping panes of glass they were carrying, painters painting a wriggly line down the center of the street instead of a straight line, things like that. I had seen enough disaster pictures to know what it probably looked like.

At this point the DeathBox started shaking violently, throwing me from one end of the box to the other.

The last thing I remember seeing before I was knocked unconscious by the constant buffeting was Fred Foster's face in the DeathBox window, mouthing the words: "You're mad, Overkill."

When I regained consciousness some time later, the first thing I noticed was that the door to the DeathBox was partway open. It had been charred black and bent almost beyond recognition.

I kicked the door completely open, and it disintegrated. Then I kicked the hell out of the DeathBox. It disintegrated too. That felt good. Scare me, will you? Burly 1, DeathBox 0.

Then I turned and saw where I was, and I regretted kicking the DeathBox to pieces. Apparently it and I were the only things left in the universe. If I hadn't kicked it to bits, at least

I wouldn't have been alone. I could have talked to the box. Now there was just me.

I was floating in limbo, all alone. The universe was gone. It had ended with a bang and a whimper. The whimper, I noticed, was coming from me.

CHAPTER FIFTEEN

It was quiet. Too quiet.
And cold. Mighty cold.
I was bobbing about in what seemed like a thin milky haze. The haze stretched as far as I could see in every direction. I didn't know where I was, but I knew instinctively that I was in the wrong place.

I started trying to get to the horizon so I could kick my way through it and get out of here. Go someplace better.

I had trouble moving through the murk at first, but after awhile I found that I could make slow progress in any direction I wanted by pointing my mouth in the opposite direction and screaming continuously. Farts, I accidentally discovered, worked also. Nothing, however, made me move very fast, so progress was slow. Not that I had anything better to do, of course, but a person likes to make good time when he's traveling.

When I got to what I had thought was the horizon, I found out it wasn't the horizon anymore. There was a new horizon now, back where I had been before. Fine. No problem. I'll go that way then. And off I farted.

It would probably be tedious reading to have to follow me through all my floating adventures. I know it seemed tedious to me when I re-read my first draft. I ended up cutting about 400 pages of it out, and I don't miss any of it. All that floating from one spot to another just bogged down the narrative, in my opinion.

So about 400 pages later, I found myself pretty much back in the same spot I had started out in. I had no idea where I was. It's all well and good to say you're in "limbo," but where the hell is that? What does it mean? Talk English! And get me out of here, while you're at it.

It's the boredom of a total void that gets to you the most. There's nobody to talk to, no magazines to read, nowhere to sit down and take a load off your feet. Nothing.

Still, I was alive, and not many people could say that, thanks to me. I found some comfort in the fact that I was the last man alive. Out of the uncounted billions who had inhabited our universe, I was the last man standing. I had won the human race.

And, of course, there are good things about being in a total void. There are no distractions, for one thing. So you can get things done, if you can find anything to do. And there are no more wars. Finally we had world peace. So, criticize me all you want, at least I got that done.

But it was still basically boring as hell.

I had my toothbrush with me, so I spent a lot

of time brushing my teeth. Nothing to eat though. Except the toothbrush. So I finally ate that.

Having some solid food in my stomach gave me a second wind. I renewed my efforts to get out of there—struggling furiously across the void, then struggling furiously back the other way. I was determined not to take "no" for an answer this time. After awhile I noticed all this struggling was wearing me out, and getting me nowhere. I had half a mind to stop struggling at this point. Maybe take "no" for an answer. Then I decided to continue struggling, but on a reduced schedule. For the next few days I would struggle for four hours in the morning, take a break for lunch (I had found another toothbrush and some car keys), then resume struggling until five. Then I'd knock off for the day.

Finally I got tired of the whole business and just quit doing anything. I just kind of laid in the void slantways looking pissed. If anyone had been watching me, they would have seen me, my hand resting on my chin, falling slowly across the void. I must have looked like a goddamn screensaver.

Okay, I just cut out another 96 pages. Mostly just stuff about me lying slantways.

Just when I was about to give up and start really lying slantways, at a much more pronounced slant, I suddenly felt an odd spinning sensation. There was nothing to reference in my surroundings, so I couldn't be sure, but I seemed to be spinning around and around, with my arms and legs outstretched, against what used to be a milky white background, but was now all stripy colored. The Time Nozzle, wherever it was, was pulling me out of this time period and sending me somewhere else!

As I spun away I heard what sounded like shrieks from Time Nozzle technicians somewhere in time saying: "He's coming right at us!" but I don't know if I was coming at them or not.

The last thing I saw—or thought I saw, I may have imagined it—before I popped out of the year 2265, was God running towards me through the void, shaking His fist angrily at me. At least I think it was God. He had the short legs and pencil thin mustache I associate with the Almighty. But before He could reach me I was gone.

Things got confused for awhile after that, as I began being thrown all over time by the plainly malfunctioning Time Nozzle.

I briefly appeared in the year 1467, where I heard someone say: "It's a witch!" And then, as I popped off again, the last thing I heard was someone saying: "It was a witch!"

I appeared in 1865, where I told Lincoln what Overkill had done, stealing his identity and oppressing the future with it, and Lincoln said it figured.

And I spent a month in 1755 Philadelphia, running a wig shop. I spent my spare time looking for Ben Franklin, so we could exchange witty remarks. I must have checked every building in that town. The guy just wasn't there. I felt that violated every rule of time traveling I had ever heard of. The big celebrity of the time period is always there. But there wasn't anybody to complain to about it, so I dropped it. But I still think it stinks. I had a terrific witty remark all ready for Franklin. He would have laughed his ass off.

Finally I arrived back in 2007 on Overkill's island.

As so often happens in time traveling—possibly because the space/time continuum likes its little joke, or, more likely, because the universe is run by a bunch of hacks—the moment I arrived back on the island was the exact moment I had walked into The Time Nozzle to try to get it to work.

I shouted at myself to "Stop! Don't go in there!" and heard myself reply: "Screw you!" I remembered saying that to somebody, but I didn't know it was me.

A few moments later I saw Fred Foster charge into The Time Nozzle after me, his arms whirling like pinwheels. This was followed by the sounds of a terrific scuffle. Then the machinery suddenly started up and thousands of future fighters raced out of The Time Nozzle into the laboratory and, with no other instructions, began to fight with everything they saw: chairs, file cabinets, pictures on the walls, even the control panel for The Time Nozzle. Then they fought their way through the door and streamed out of the fortress to fight with the world.

I had planned to wait until the coast was clear and then operate The Time Nozzle controls to bring myself back, so there would be two of me here. Then the world had better look out. I could work two jobs then. Make twice as much money.

But when I got down from the light fixture I was hanging from and took a look at The Time Nozzle, I saw that it had been pretty much smashed to pieces. It was just a worthless piece of TV memorabilia now.

I wished somebody had smashed it sooner.

CHAPTER SIXTEEN

I had expected there to be a lot of fighting going on outside the fortress, but things were relatively quiet now. The only fighting that was going on when I got out there was between the future fighters and various inanimate objects. While they furiously attacked statues, palm trees, and sprinkler systems, the government troops and my Unholy Army hid behind bushes together, waiting for the newcomers to leave so they could go back to killing each other. It was too dangerous to kill each other out there right now.

I tried to make my way past the future fighters to the water without being seen, but I'm not as stealthy as I'd like to be. Maybe if I lost some weight I'd be stealthier. Or maybe I need to gain a lot more weight. Anyway, they spotted me in about five seconds.

They started coming towards me. I wondered if they knew that I was the one who had brought them here and was responsible for them getting their great medical plans. I tried giving them an order.

"Halt!" I commanded.

They kept coming. I tried another order.

"Stop looking at me like that!"

Their expressions didn't change.

I turned to run and bumped violently into a huge metal Picasso sculpture that Overkill had stolen from Chicago. It collapsed into a million pieces. The future fighters stopped, stunned. They had been trying to bust up that statue for hours. As I said earlier, it's all about not being balanced properly.

With me leading the way, we tore up that island six ways from Sunday. They made way for me whenever something particularly valuable needed to be destroyed. I was quite enjoying myself and thinking of maybe staying a little longer and going home in the morning. But good sense finally prevailed. I suddenly broke for the water and entered it in a low flat dive, sank quickly to the bottom, then struggled back up to the surface. I had forgotten that I didn't know how to swim. I remembered it now, though. The bottom of the lake reminded me.

Fortunately, the water was filled with floating debris and handy corpses to hang onto. The future fighters had ripped up the attacking ships as easily as they had ripped up everything else and the surface of the lake was more debris than water. You could practically walk on it. I slowly and carefully worked my way to shore.

Central City was a total mess. The future fighters were all over the streets, pushing over buildings, punching out streetlights, tipping over trucks and cars, eating the pavement, stamping policemen flat, and tearing newspapermen to shreds.

A few hardy souls were trying to fight back, firing at the invaders, but the bullets not only didn't stop them, the invaders actually caught the bullets and ate them. One future fighter liked the taste so much he picked up an abandoned rifle and emptied the entire clip down his throat. People stopped firing guns at them after that. There didn't seem to be much point in feeding the creatures.

When I saw all the mindless destruction going on, I didn't hesitate. I joined right in, once again impressing the future fighters with my superior ability to destroy. You know that 600 foot tall revolving restaurant in the center of town? I destroyed that. Just leaned on it while I was eating a sandwich. Impressed the hell out of the guys.

We made our way through town, trashing everything in sight. When we got near my house, I split from my group, supposedly to destroy a dark alley I said had been asking for it. I hid in the alley until the future fighters got tired of waiting for me and moved on, then I headed for home.

A few streets from my house, the Mayor and the Police Commissioner spotted me and came running towards me, yelling at me to get to work and stop this invasion. The way they had it figured out, I still owed the city four and a half days work. And they expected me to live up to my obligations. Before I could give them and the horse they rode in on my answer, they disappeared down the gullet of a future fighter. So I guess they have more important things to worry about now than my contract. Digestive juices, and so on.

I was relieved to find that my house hadn't been damaged so far. The scary footprints all over the floors made it plain that the future fighters had been there, but nothing had been disturbed. The place had always looked trashed, so anybody looking to destroy something would think somebody had already been there and beaten them to it and move on to the next house.

Several times that evening I heard future fighters approach the house, look in the door, then grunt and leave, as I sat there reading my smelly newspaper in my own filth. Okay, so I ain't neat. But at least nobody bothered my place.

The city fathers didn't know what to do to stop the invasion. They tried raising their own salaries, but that didn't do any good. They tried it again. Still no luck. At that point they just raised their salaries a couple more times and fled. The police weren't any help either. They refused to come out of their police stations. Wouldn't even answer their phone. So nobody in authority was doing anything to stop the carnage.

I suppose you're waiting for me to fix all this—make it so everything is back the way it was before. I know my mother is. But it isn't going to happen.

I tried to figure out a way to do it. For awhile I assumed The Time Nozzle would eventually pop the future fighters back to the future, and I could take credit for it, maybe run for office on the strength of it, but then I remembered wrecking the 2265 end of the tunnel. And the future fighters had wrecked the end located in this time period. So I don't think we can expect any help from The Time Nozzle on this one.

And I don't think there's anything The Flying Detective can do. This doesn't look like a job for him. I don't have my costume anymore, anyway. The last time I saw it, one of the future fighters was parading around town in it.

I ran into the Devil a couple of days ago, when we both happened to be downtown leaning up against lamp posts. He said he could fix everything up for me just like it was before. The world would be saved and I would be everyone's hero. But I decided against it. He wanted a little too much in return. He wanted my soul and the highest I would go was my personality. He didn't want that. So we didn't have a deal.

So I'm out of ideas. Maybe the whole thing will blow over someday. Most things do. Let's hope so, anyway. Oh, and sorry. Sorry, everyone.

One last thing before I go. During my travels through time I showed up briefly in 2266 and 2264 and there was a universe in both time periods. Just not one in 2265. If I knew more about how these things worked I'd let you know, but as near as I can figure, when December 31st, 2264 rolls around, we're all going to have to jump.